The Last of Her Lies

A Maggie Garrett Mystery

Jean Taylor

Seal Press

Library of Congress Cataloging-in Publication Data
Taylor, Jean
The last of her lies / Jean Taylor
I. Title
PS3570.A935L3   1996   813'.54—dc20   95-50395
ISBN: 1-878067-75-3

Printed in the United States of America
First printing, March 1996
10 9 8 7 6 5 4 3 2 1

Distributed to the trade by Publishers Group West
In Canada: Publishers Group West Canada, Toronto, Canada
In Europe and the U.K.: Airlift Book Company, London, England

Cover and text design by Clare Conrad
Cover photograph by Elizabeth Mangelsdorf

Acknowledgments

Heartfelt thanks to my fabulous manuscript reader/critiquers (with a few special awards of merit): Jim Mitulski & Bob Crocker (for your generosity of spirit and for those wonderfully twisted novels you loan me), Janya Lalich & Kim Vickers, Jill Langston (for scouting crime locations and photography), Jaem Heath-O'Ryan, Jan Adams & Rebecca Gordon, Bob D'Arcy, Cherie James, Steve Marlowe, Dana Topping, Sharon Stover, René Richard, Laurie Gordon and Suzanne Dumont (my real-life therapists/advisors), Bill Hellendale, and Robin Stevens (for indulging my second-novel anxieties).

Cyber kisses to the volunteer staff and regulars of Lambda Rising Rainbow Cafe on America Online (especially Carole Taylor, Semi Moore, Great Toes, Nightwmn, Dor 28 and our boyfriend Shagalon). You are the closest I'm likely to get to an "organized" writers' support group.

Special thanks to my editors, Barbara Wilson and June Thomas.

Dedicated to Angela, Carol and Mark:
the therapists who helped me get over.

Cast Of Characters

MAGGIE GARRETT, sole proprietor of Windsor & Garrett, Private Investigations

RICARDO GALVÉZ, Maggie's office staff

LIAM O'MEARA, Maggie's closest friend

JESSIE GIULIANI, Maggie's other closest friend, executive secretary, cancer activist, meddler

TATE PRITCHARD, Jessie's lover, Maggie's friend, psychotherapist

SERGEANT DIANA HOFFMAN, San Francisco Police Department, Homicide Section; Maggie's current romantic interest

CHAD OSAFUNE, friend of Maggie's, operative at Glass Security Agency

MOIRA ERICSON, psychotherapist accused of exploiting one of her clients

KELLY HENRY, missing woman whom Maggie is hired to find; left behind a journal that accuses Moira Ericson of sexually abusing her

SYLVIA ERICSON, Moira's stepmother

HOWARD ERICSON, Moira's father

ROBERT SUMMERS, the Ericsons' attorney

LISA (a.k.a. MARY BETH DANIELS), runaway who lives in the house where Kelly Henry lived

PHYLLIS TRAWICK, high school teacher

AL WELLINGTON, "landlord" of the flophouse where Kelly Henry lived

JERRY REARDON, manager of Nature's Harmony Foods

CHAPTER ONE

August 23. Today when I got to her office she showed me her new couch. She folded it out, so it made a bed. Then she sat down on it and told me it was time I committed to my sexuality. She said therapy was a safe place to do that and she was there to help me. I started crying, and she asked what stake I had in being sick. I ran outside and sat by her door for awhile. Then I went back in. She said when I was ready to get well, I should let her know.

"Tate, is this real? Where did you get it?" I dropped the piece of paper onto my desk and met my friend's warm brown eyes.

"It's copied from a journal. I wish I knew if it's for real. The young woman who wrote it disappeared two weeks ago."

"And you want me to find her?"

"No . . . It's complicated. I was asked to approach you by the family of the therapist in the journal."

"I don't get it. Why would they ask you?"

"I've known the therapist for a long time. Her name is Moira Ericson."

"You *know* her? I can't believe it. You couldn't be friends with somebody who'd exploit a client that way!"

Tate gave me that therapist look. The one that says, "My, what a strong reaction. Could it remind you of something else? Perhaps we should explore it."

What she said aloud was: "Easy, Maggie, I didn't say that Moira and I were friends. We went through postgraduate training together, and we do have friends—and a lot of history—in common."

"So this therapist, Moira," I forced myself to say her name, "came to you when her client went missing?"

"No, it was an attorney who represents Moira's family. You used to work in law firms, you might have heard of him—Robert Summers." I certainly had heard the name. Milton, Halburton, Branfield & Summers was the second-largest firm in San Francisco.

"They must be rich if Summers is running errands for them!"

"I think you're right. Moira's parents live in Arizona. When they heard that the police were questioning Moira about Kelly Henry (that's the woman who wrote the journal), they came here, and they're planning to stay until Moira gets cleared. Robert Summers represents the family in business, and I got the impression that he was only involved in this as a personal favor."

"Where do I come in?"

"Moira's a lesbian. According to the attorney, Kelly's sexuality is a mystery, but she has gay connections. The family already hired one detective agency, but they didn't learn much. So the Ericsons decided to find someone from 'our community,' as Mr. Summers put it. He asked me if I knew of anyone, and of course I told him about you."

"Who would my client be?"

"The Ericson family. If you're willing to take the job, they'd like you to come to their hotel and meet with them."

"What about Moira? Where does she fit into all this?"

Tate stared out my rather grimy window. "Mr. Summers said that Moira claims she's done nothing wrong. Other than giving my name to her family, she won't have anything to do with the investigation. I haven't even talked to her. It sounds as if she's in denial about the whole thing."

"Tate, what do you think? Could Moira have done this to a client?"

"I honestly don't know, and, believe me, I've given it plenty of thought. Before I called you I did some online research. I found a few studies of therapists who have sex with their clients. A fairly high percentage of male therapists get involved with their clients at some point during their careers, but few women therapists do. I couldn't find anything on lesbian therapists, but I suspect the rate would be even lower than for straight women."

"But this isn't about having sex with a client. This is about telling a woman that she can't get well unless she gets into the therapist's bed."

"You're right. This behavior," she tapped the page with a blunt fingertip, "is outlaw behavior. If it's for real, Moira should never be allowed to see another client. I don't think she *would* do this kind of thing, but I can't guarantee that she's the heroine of the story either." We looked at each other for half a minute. Finally she spoke again. "Do you want to meet the Ericsons?"

"Well, I'm not exactly over-busy at the moment. The rent on this office is going up again, and I've got to get new tires for the surveillance van."

"That's crap, Maggie. You want to find out what really happened between those two women."

"Okay, that too, which you knew would happen if you showed me this journal. But I *do* have bills to pay. So the upshot is, yes, I'd love to meet the Ericsons."

"I hope getting you involved with the case isn't a mistake." Now that Tate had achieved her purpose, she was back-pedaling. "Jessie will kill me if this gets messy for you."

She was right. Jessie is Tate's life partner, and my best friend. If the job turned out to be a horror show, Jessie wouldn't let Tate forget about it, and the image of a wrathful Jessie was enough to give anyone pause.

"You brought me the case, for which I thank you. That's where your responsibility ends," I said, with the curious sensation of playing therapist to Tate.

She smiled ruefully as she let herself out of my office: "Why do I not believe that?"

CHAPTER TWO

Robert Summers' secretary put me through right away when I gave her my name, quite a rush for someone who drudged for years as a temporary legal assistant for $400-an-hour men like him.

Summers asked me to meet him at the Ericsons' suite at the Fairmont that afternoon. I managed to finagle an extra hour to dash home and change. You don't meet clients at the Fairmont wearing a T-shirt and old jeans. But then again, my plan for the day had been cleaning my office, and I'd been up to my elbows in Ajax when Tate arrived.

The Flood Building cleaning staff do what they can in the ten minutes that the building management allocates for the offices of Windsor & Garrett, Private Investigations (that's me), but this historic landmark gets plenty of dust through its loose, historic windows. Occasionally the accumulated grittiness that drifts in from Market Street drives me to action.

It might help business if I moved to the Castro District, closer to my clientele (mostly gay men and lesbians), but I'd miss coming to work at this weird urban circus. The Cable Car Turnaround, a magnet for tourists, is a few steps away. Street preachers, panhandlers, performers and artisans vie for the attention of the hundreds of people queued up for the next car. Shoppers from the 'burbs come for the sales at Macy's, The Emporium and Nordstrom. A lot of countries have consulates in the Flood Building, and protesters frequently greet me when I come back from lunch. My pockets are always stuffed with flyers denouncing the latest human rights outrage in Peru or El Salvador. The block has been brought a bit closer to midwestern shopping mall with the addition of a Gap store and Mayor Pickering's war on the homeless, but it's still my beloved nutcase San Francisco.

I left a note for my one-man office staff, Ricardo Galvéz, in case he made it in that day, and jogged the three blocks to the parking lot for my car. On days like this it's worth paying extra for a spot that's always accessible without moving a dozen other cars.

Within minutes I was at my cottage in Noe Valley. The animals with whom I share this doll-sized house looked startled and faintly guilty when I walked in midafternoon, confirming my paranoid imaginings of what they really do while I'm gone all day. I did a quick inspection of the premises, but found no structural damage. They followed on my heels, making half-hearted requests for feeding and walking, but none of us took it seriously.

The cats, Fearless and Pod, are constants in my life, more dependable in their affection and frequently more entertaining than my string of ex-lovers. Somehow, we always have at least one additional animal around. Pugsley is the latest. He is of course a pug, the pushiest in dogdom. His owner died a few months ago, and the man who inherited him has been traveling, so I'm doing foster care until his return. Although Pugsley and I had been friends for years, behavior that is charming in a visitor is a very different story in a live-in. To date, I'd compiled twenty synonyms for "insufferable."

I showered and tried to remember which blouse was clean/ironed/color-coordinated with my one clean skirt. None of them, it turned out, but if I kept my jacket on, the pale yellow silk with the mysterious stain on the shoulder would do.

One pair of pantyhose remained in their package in my sock drawer. I soon discovered why they were unworn. The package said Tall, but the hose were Petite. I'm 5' 11". I hurled the stubby things into a far corner of the room, where Fearless pounced on them. With fierce growls, she tore them to shreds and brought them back to lay at my feet. I praised her, and threw them for her to subdue again. It was a terrible precedent to set, but I did enjoy pantyhose slaughter. I dug through my handwashing pile and found a pair that didn't smell bad. A notoriously nondomestic friend claims that if you wait long enough, your dirty clothes become wearable again. Looked like it was true. Two terrible precedents in one afternoon.

Three minutes left for hair and makeup. Years ago a hairdresser enamored of my carrot red hair persuaded me to model for a hairdressing competition in exchange for a free haircut. That's how I got the bold, asymmetrical style that I've kept even though everyone else has stopped wearing it. The downside is that without a monthly trim I start looking strange instead of sleek, and I was way overdue. I slathered on styling gel and hoped for the best. Next, makeup: dark green eye liner that a former lover swore turned my eyes into emerald pools, and mascara for that sophisticated sleuth effect. A little blusher to reassure everyone that I was alive, lipstick that would be gone with my next cup of coffee, a splash of Hermes' Equipage to cover any remaining hint of Pine-Sol, and I was out the door.

CHAPTER THREE

I made it to the Ericsons' hotel with a minute to spare. The haughty uniformed individual in the lobby gave qualified approval to my efforts at respectability and pointed at the elevator to the Ericsons' suite.

At first glance, Howard Ericson and Robert Summers were interchangeable: white men, 50ish, medium-height, gym-conditioned, well-dressed and barbered. Unlike Summers, however, Ericson was quite ill at ease. His hands were shoved into his pockets, distorting the excellent cut of his jacket. He made no attempt to hide his dismay when I introduced myself to the two of them.

"Ms. Garrett? I was expecting someone older and more, uh—"

I longed to supply the word he seemed to be searching for: "butch." I didn't, but neither was I inclined to ease his discomfort. What a shame I hadn't worn lace.

Summers stepped into the breach. "I had our human resources department check your references, Ms. Garrett, and I was quite impressed," he said, and shot me a lawyer glare. Translation: "Yes, the man's a fool, but this is business, so play nice." Summers gestured toward the sofa, and said, "We're just waiting for Mrs. Ericson to join us. Please make yourself comfortable, Ms. Garrett."

I perched on the edge of the deep-dish leather couch. Ericson paced nervously. Every third or fourth pass around the room, he'd take a gulp from a glass on the table. Several times I noticed him staring at me.

It was tempting to stare right back at him. This was the father of a therapist accused of tricking a defenseless woman into paying for her own sexual abuse. I put the brakes on this train of thought and kept my eyes on the suite's reproductions of eighteenth-century prints.

A hotel maid wheeled in a full-fledged English tea. Ericson pulled himself together and acted as host. I took what I presumed to be a ladylike portion of this array. My femme presentation was throwing my client into confusion, and that was too much fun to blow by indulging in my natural gluttony.

My sandwich choice was a disappointment (watercress-like green matter and unidentifiable beige pâté), and I was looking for a discreet place to get rid of it when an elegant, fashionably emaciated woman entered the room.

Sylvia Ericson might be anywhere from her late thirties to her early fifties. Her skin had the tautness produced by relentless facial surgery. She wore her pale blonde hair chin-length, pushed behind her ears to display diamond earrings that would make my drag-queen friends swoon. A lifetime of surreptitious *Vogue*-reading supplied the word "pyjamas" to describe her attire: elaborate loungewear, which no one actually wears for sleeping. Her full-cut navy velvet top floated over matching wide velvet pants as she walked.

With a slight frown she surveyed the contents of the tea tray and adjusted a precariously balanced plate. Then she approached the couch where I was sitting and extended her hand.

"Hello, you must be Ms. Garrett. I'm Sylvia Ericson." Her voice was low and seductive, and I was getting the full treatment.

"Now that we're all here, why don't we discuss the matter at hand," Summers said. He had polished off two crème pastries and was dabbing telltale traces from his upper lip.

11

"Do you know my daughter, Ms. Garrett?" asked Ericson. He pulled a silver case from his pocket and started to take out a cigarette, but a murmured protest from his wife made him put it away.

"No, I've never met her." I considered asking him whether he thought all the lesbians in San Francisco knew each other. Time for an attitude check. These people were paying for my time. Think about the rent, the tires and the insurance payment coming due.

"I wish Moira would cooperate," Sylvia Ericson said. "This is so awkward. I'm sure she could give you much more background than we can."

"Yes, well, she's not cooperating," growled Ericson. "She's acting like a damned adolescent! If we have to go through with this, let's get on with it!" He hadn't bothered to conceal his skepticism about me. Now he sounded like a reluctant party to the investigation altogether.

Summers moved in smoothly to take over. "Ms. Garrett, the Ericsons wish to employ you to look into the circumstances of Kelly Henry's disappearance. There is no doubt in their minds that the diary she left behind is either a hoax or the product of a seriously disturbed imagination. Naturally, they hope that you will locate Ms. Henry alive and well. If, on the other hand, Ms. Henry has met with an accident or misfortune, they wish to uncover any facts that will corroborate their daughter's innocence."

"How long has Kelly Henry been missing?" My question was addressed to the Ericsons, who looked as startled as if the tea tray had spoken.

"She's been gone two weeks," Summers, the designated talker, said. "She didn't show up for either of her jobs on the eighteenth of last month, nor did she attend her therapy session that same day. Moira told me that she became concerned because Ms. Henry

12

had never missed a session. Ms. Henry had no phone, so Moira went to the house where Ms. Henry rented a room. It's a nest of illegal aliens, deviants and drug-users, and no one had noticed that she was gone. At that point Moira called the police."

In contrast to his formal usage with all of us, Summers referred to Moira Ericson by her first name. Was that because he had known her since her childhood, or did he see this woman, who must be at least thirty-five years old, as a child?

Summers paused and turned to the Ericsons to give them a chance to comment. Neither chose to do so. Sylvia Ericson gazed thoughtfully at the half-moons of her perfect nail tips. Howard Ericson had resumed his pacing. His eyes never left his wife. Summers took in all of this and continued, his narrative polished by years of performance before judge and jury.

"The police searched Ms. Henry's room and found a notebook, presumably kept by her, in which bizarre allegations of sexual abuse and professional misconduct are made against Moira. The police were more interested in this notebook than in finding Ms. Henry herself. Apart from demanding that Moira disclose confidential client information, they appear to have done very little. We do know through other sources that Ms. Henry hasn't returned to her room."

"How do you know that?"

"We've had twenty-four-hour surveillance on the house. In addition to yourself, we have secured the services of the Glass Security Agency. They can handle that sort of thing, provide the muscle—"

Ericson interrupted: "What we want you to focus on is talking to Ms. Henry's contemporaries, since you as a, uh . . . ." He fumbled for words that conveyed 'dyke who presumably consorts with drug users and other perverts,' but would avoid saying it outright.

Summers beamed me a warning glare. One of my references

13

must have mentioned my temper.

"You're right, Mr. Ericson," I said, and tried to visualize new brake linings. "They are more likely to talk to me than to anyone at Glass."

"I'm pleased that we understand each other," Summers purred.

"Do you want to discuss the terms of my contract now?"

"Let's spare the Ericsons those details. They've been under a great deal of strain."

"I do have a few questions about the scope of my work." Summers nodded for me to continue. "I realize that Moira isn't participating in this investigation, but I wonder if I might try talking to her. There may be things, even within the bounds of confidentiality, that she could tell me—"

"Not at this time," Summers cut me off. "As Mrs. Ericson said, our efforts are proceeding against Moira's expressed wishes. The family sees no purpose in antagonizing her further by delving into her personal and professional life until we have exhausted all other avenues of inquiry. Concentrate on finding Ms. Henry."

"Do *not* contact my daughter," Howard Ericson said angrily. "The police have dragged her through hell already. I will not have her harassed any further!" His face was red. Sylvia Ericson gently placed her hand on his sleeve. He gave a long sigh and relaxed slightly.

Sylvia turned to me. "Howard is very protective of his daughter," she said. "We understand that this may make your investigation more difficult, but it is crucial that Moira not be disturbed."

"I see," I lied. I didn't see the point at all. "Well, then, I guess all that's left is for me to get any other information you already have on Kelly Henry. For example, do you have a copy of her entire journal?"

Summers put down his tea abruptly, sloshing it onto the fine linen tea cloth. He glanced at both Ericsons, who pointedly did not meet his eyes. He cleared his throat and squared his shoulders.

"Yes, Ms. Garrett, there is a copy, which I have had duplicated for you. It was obtained by the other security agency, by what I suspect were unorthodox, if not illegal, means." No wonder he was flustered. Men like Summers do not often find themselves having to discuss petty bribery or outright theft. "While I realize you need it for your investigation, I would ask that you keep tight control over it and return it when your work is completed. Is that understood?"

"I understand. Did you have any questions for me?" I asked the Ericsons.

"No, if Summers here says you're qualified, that's good enough for me," Howard Ericson responded. "And anyway, we have the other agency to do the heavy work. Go to it, Ms. Garrett."

"My husband is delightfully old-fashioned," Sylvia said. "He thinks we women have to be taken care of, and I'm afraid I let him believe it. I'm sure that, if necessary, you could handle all of it yourself, Maggie—may I call you Maggie? But we want you to be able to give this your special attention. The other agency will merely be supporting your efforts."

This woman was obviously used to saving her husband from his social gaffes. She stepped close and took both my hands in hers. Her eyes widened in a heart-stopping manner that must have required many hours of practice. Damn, it worked.

"We simply want to make this go away for Moira," she said. "Moira has had a difficult life, but she has rebuffed all of our attempts to help her. This is one thing we *can* do for her. Please find this Henry girl for us, and we'll both be so grateful."

I found myself wanting to assure her that I'd take care of everything, just as, no doubt, everyone else did.

"I apologize if I've caused any offense, Ms. Garrett," Ericson said curtly, his eyes directed everywhere except at me. "I know Moira is a grown woman, but to me she's still my little girl. I'm worried about her, and I haven't been myself. Please help us." His voice was gruff with emotion.

"I'll do my best, Mr. Ericson." We shook hands again, and when our eyes met, I thought that for the first time each of us saw another full human being, not the caricatures of an overly rich straight man and a low-rent dyke P.I.

"One last thing," I said. "Ms. Ericson, you spoke of Moira as your husband's daughter. You're her stepmother?"

"Please call me Sylvia. Yes, Moira's mother died when Moira was still in her teens. I married Howard the following year. Moira was . . . unable to accept our marriage." The pain caused by such implacable opposition crossed her face briefly, then as quickly was gone.

The Ericsons left, and Summers and I took care of the contractual details. Then he handed me a large check to cover initial expenses and a folder of reports from the Glass Agency. We agreed that he would receive my first report in two days, and I was on the job.

CHAPTER FOUR

May 16. I went to the Women's Therapy Center today. They gave me a long form to fill out, and I had my intake interview. They said I can go there five times on the sliding scale. If I still need help after that, they'll try to get me a long-term referral. Then I got to talk to a therapist. She was really nice. Her name is Moira Ericson. She said I could call her Moira. I felt like things might get better for the first time in a long time.

June 9. I only have one more session with Moira left, and I'm getting kind of nervous. I like her, I can trust her. She cares about me. What if she won't keep seeing me? She says it's against the Therapy Center's rules. If I keep seeing her, we have to keep it a secret. I got another job selling tickets to the Symphony over the phone. Maybe I can make enough to pay her.

June 13. Moira told me she will keep seeing me, and that I need to see her at least twice a week. She said $50 for each visit is a low rate. The calls at the Symphony have been okay, but there's nothing left after rent and food. Still, I know it will all work out somehow.

June 14. I had an exit interview at the Therapy Center. Moira told me what to tell them. I said it had been helpful and that I was okay and didn't need to see anybody anymore. That way they won't find out that she is breaking the rules. Tomorrow is my first session in her office!

The major item in the folder Robert Summers had given me was a third-generation photocopy of Kelly Henry's journal. "Journal" made it sound like one of those precious leather- or cloth-bound books I've never seen anyone use. Kelly had written in a spiral notebook, the cheap kind you can buy anywhere.

The narrative started a couple of months before Kelly's first session with Moira, the therapist she was assigned at the Women's Therapy Center, and ended two days before she disappeared.

The early entries were intermittent: a dismal account of a young woman's arrival in San Francisco and her search for work, a place to live, and the kind of human connections that frequently elude newcomers. She found a part-time job as a stock person at a health food store, and moved into a room in the Mission District. She described relentless depression. In May, Kelly made her first visit to the Women's Therapy Center. After that the entries became more frequent, almost daily. All of the entries were about Moira.

There was little else in the folder about Kelly. The only photo of her was a badly focused group shot, taken in front of Nature's Harmony Foods, the store where she had worked.

Someone had circled Kelly's face, but even without the crude blue marker, she stood out in the photograph. A tall, middle-aged man was positioned behind her, smiling broadly into the camera. He held Kelly's small hands aloft. With his free hand he was untying her hair from its pony tail. Kelly was leaning away from him, and from the others, her face partially hidden by her upraised arms. Two of the other women in the photo watched the struggle with amusement. Everyone else was ignoring the big man and Kelly. I shivered. It was a kind of public rape.

I pulled a magnifying glass out of the drawer to get a better look at Kelly. She had delicate features in a triangular face. Her hair was heavy and glossy. Even in the bad photo she stood out as a beautiful woman.

"Hi Maggie. We got a new case?" Ricardo banged his way into the office. Employing a high school junior has many drawbacks: pre-exam jitters, anxiety about how his college tuition will be paid, insecurity about what exactly is involved in becoming a man. I'm not much help on any of those fronts, although I do pay better than Burger King.

Ricardo's mother Alicia is an old friend, and I've watched him and his siblings grow up. After he installed the software on my computer as a weekend job over a year ago, he somehow never left. Alicia's only knowledge of private investigators comes from TV, and she worries about her brilliant son getting hurt or, more likely, getting into trouble because of his delight in hacking into forbidden computer files. Alicia does agree that working for me beats the dangers of gangs and drugs awaiting an idle seventeen-year-old in San Francisco's Mission District. The atmosphere at Windsor & Garrett is closer to that of the family-run dry cleaners in my neighborhood than a typical office.

"Hi, so glad you could make it!"

"Come on, Maggie, I told you I'd be late today. Mom made me take Tía Gloria to the foot clinic to interpret for her. I think the real reason Mom makes me go is to shame Tía into staying 'til her appointment. Otherwise, if they tell her she has to wait five minutes, she gets up and goes home, and then she tells my mom the doctor died, and the clinic is closed. Is that coffee as old as it smells?"

"Older. Go ahead and start a new pot, and then sit down. I'm going to need lots of help on this one. The Glass Security guys have been working on it for days, but all they've done is throw the Ericsons' money around to get a copy of the missing woman's journal and watch her house—they've got zip on her. I think we'll need to start from the beginning, as if it were a brand new case."

I filled him in on my interview with the Ericsons, gave him the photo of Kelly to have copied, and set him to checking on Kelly's background through our standard routes: Department of Motor Vehicles, utilities, employers. He waited for me to leave the room to begin. Ricardo can sound just like a woman on the phone, which always elicits a more favorable response from bureaucrats. This process demands locked doors, since Ricardo will only perform his cross-gender vocalizing in private. His peers would make his life a misery if they knew about it.

In my part of the "suite," I set up files on the investigation, paid the most pressing bills and prepared a deposit slip for the Ericsons' check. Then I read another substantial chunk of Kelly's journal. When I looked up again, an hour and a half had gone by, and my revulsion on reading the first page felt like nothing compared to the effect of immersing myself in the day-by-day history of a trusting woman's betrayal.

I couldn't sit in the office another minute. On the way out I said good-bye to Ricardo. His body was seated at the computer in the front office, but he was riding the modem to new territories. He grunted something without removing his face from the monitor. I hoped he wasn't accessing illegal materials. Since he probably was, I hoped he wouldn't get caught. At the last minute I stuck the rest of the journal pages in my bag to take home.

The heat of the late-afternoon sun and the rush-hour chaos of Market Street brought me out of the gloom that had dropped down on me while I read Kelly's journal. By the time I reached the parking garage I felt energetic enough to check out the health food store where Kelly had worked.

Nature's Harmony Foods was on Judah Street in the Inner

Sunset District. The neighborhood was part old-time residents, part students from the nearby medical school, and part young clerical grinds from the Financial District. Each time I visited friends in the neighborhood, another business catering to people with disposable incomes and upscale tastes had opened.

I parked and dug paper bags out of the trunk, knowing it would be a bring-your-own-containers operation. Shopping made a good cover, and I could always replace the vegetable matter rotting in the fridge. Freshly roasted coffee beckoned me from a gourmet coffee store that used to be a shoe-repair shop. I resisted, promising myself a cup after Nature's Harmony.

I prowled the aisles for a few minutes. The display of goods was haphazard: organic toothpaste next to rye flakes. Cleanliness didn't seem to be a high priority either. How did they pass health inspections? Taking home any of the bulk produce would be inviting insect infestations: bins of flour and esoteric grains were uncovered, and flies buzzed around the spigots of honey and syrup kegs. A grubby three-year-old ran his hands through a granola bin, ignoring the half-hearted protests of his mother, who was comparing labels on organic wines. Maybe I'd confine my purchases to stuff in sealed containers.

The place was full of rush-hour shoppers picking up dinner ingredients. I made my way to the books and pamphlets section in the back, which gave a view of much of the store. I thumbed through brochures on fat-burning enzymes and enhancing the immune system via macrobiotics, and watched the action.

Although I had counted half a dozen employees, there were only two cashiers at the checkout counter. They were deconstructing a performance piece both had seen the night before, and their rate of ringing up purchases was, at best, leisurely. The line of customers grew. I laughed out loud when three customers raised their wrists in synchronized motion to consult their watches and then shook their heads in disgust.

A first-timer to the store rashly strode right up to one of the cashiers, without noticing the single line of people queued up behind a tall shelf to the left. Wordlessly the cashier pointed to the painted arrow on the floor. The other customers glared at the chastened man as he slunk to the end of the queue.

After I had pretended to read a yellowed treatise on the evils of mucus for about ten minutes, a large man loomed at my side. I recognized him as the gorilla who had been all over Kelly in the photo.

"May I help you find something, miss?" He was standing too close. I could smell his unwashed hair, and his breath reeked of wine.

"Oh, no, thanks. I'm just browsing."

"Well, the books are for sale. We can't let people read things here, like it was a library." His thin hair was red, turning gray, his nose a strawberry set on burst-vein cheeks. He reminded me of Bud, a field hand who worked for my dad on sober days.

"Of course, I'm sorry, I was trying to get up the nerve to ask for the manager." I hadn't planned to make my move this soon, but what the hell.

"Why do you want to see him?"

"I'm a graduate student at San Francisco State. My marketing instructor says this is one of the best-run stores in the Bay Area, and since I was in the neighborhood this afternoon, I dropped in."

"Well, why didn't you say so? I'm the manager, Jerry Reardon." He wiped his hand on his pants before shaking mine.

"Hi, I'm Maggie Garrett."

"Best-run, you say?"

"I was so excited by what I saw when I got inside, that, well, here I am." It is almost impossible to lay it on too thick with some people. Jerry was one of those people. His demeanor changed from righteous storekeeper to flattered adolescent male.

"Aren't you the sweetest thing? Why don't you come back to my office?" Jerry guided me through the Employees Only door to the tiny room he called his office. I perched carefully on the rickety folding chair he placed next to his and turned down his offer of canned ice tea. There was an empty wine bottle in his wastebasket. Not the expensive organic stuff from the shelves outside.

"Tell me again what you're studying," he said.

"Alternative Retail Administration. Have you heard of it?"

"I think so, yeah, now that you mention it."

"It's a fairly new program." Real new, I just made it up. "Alternative Retail doesn't get as much publicity as the mainstream business administration courses, but students who are committed to places like this manage to find it. Anyway, I need to do a volunteer internship with an alternative business, so I can see how it works in the real world."

"Intern, you say. What would I have to do?" I could see his thought processes swarming all over "volunteer."

"Oh, fill out a couple of evaluation forms for me at the end of the internship. The school tries to make it as painless as possible. They know how many responsibilities men like you have already. I'm sorry, I don't have the referral letter from my faculty advisor with me, but . . ."

"When do you want to start?" Was he eying my biceps or my breasts?

"I could start tomorrow if you wanted, though I realize you probably have to check with the owner and get my references . . . ."

"No, I'm the manager, it's my decision," he announced, "and I think it's a great idea. Come in at eight tomorrow."

"That's fantastic! But do you think we could make it ten o'clock? I have a class at eight."

"Sure. Just ask for me when you get in."

"Thank you so much!" As he shook my right hand, Jerry slid

his left hand lightly down my arm. I moved away and out the door fast, holding to my side the arm that was determined to reach out and whack him. This might turn out to be the shortest undercover gig of all time.

CHAPTER FIVE

I was heading for the cappuccino I had promised myself when a car horn blast from close by made me leap into the air. I spun around to glare at the culprit and saw Howard Ericson at the wheel of a silver-grey Saab idling at the curb.

"Maggie—Miss, uh, Ms. Garrett, I'm sorry if I frightened you. I wondered if we could talk for a few minutes." He grinned apologetically.

"All right, how about that coffee shop?"

"No, there's no privacy in a place like that, and you're sitting hip-to-hip with freaks." He unlocked the door on the passenger side and gestured for me to get in.

"I'm driving, too. My car's around the corner. I know a quiet place where we can talk." Mom would be proud. No way was I getting into his car.

I explained how to get to a restaurant/bar in my Noe Valley neighborhood. Ericson cut off another car to enter traffic, and then had to brake for a careless pedestrian. Ericson leaned on the horn and shook his fist as the man scrambled onto the sidewalk.

As I circled around the neighborhood for a legal parking place, I tried to pinpoint what it was about Howard Ericson that made me anxious about meeting him within ten blocks of my house, aside from the fact that he appeared to have followed me. How would I describe him to Jessie? All the terms that I could justifiably use made him sound like a generic pompous-ass business-man—in other words, like dozens of the attorneys at Jessie's law firm. But it wasn't his wealth, or his stereotypical attitudes toward women in general and lesbians in particular that gave me the creeps. He seemed to be just barely maintaining control over— what? Anger, fear, plain old executive stress? What might happen if he lost control?

"This is silly, he's your client," I told myself. "Get a grip, girl, you could take him if you had to." I found a parking place that was a little short, and trusted that the homeowner wasn't feeling vindictive.

Ericson was at the bar already and halfway through his drink when I entered the restaurant. I ordered coffee and watched him fumble with several matches before he succeeded in lighting his cigarette.

"Are you sure you don't want something else in that coffee?" he asked, with an uneasy "har, har" approximation of a laugh.

"Thanks, but I'll be on your payroll tonight, and I need to stay alert. Investigators don't work nine to five. What can I do for you, Mr. Ericson?"

"I'm, uh, sorry if we got off on the wrong foot today. I meant what I said. If Bob Summers says you're the best, that's good enough for me, whatever, er, persuasion you may be."

"Thank you," I replied, willing him to get the subliminal message that "Thank" was not my verb of choice.

"What I wanted to talk to you about is—I want you to report anything you find to me, separately, before you do your official report to Summers." He paused for a reaction, which I was careful not to show. "I, uh, want a chance to edit out any material that may not be suitable for my wife to be exposed to."

"I understand," I said, trying not to sound too gloomy, and took a deep drink of the stale bar coffee. This meant more one-on-ones with Ericson.

"I doubt that you do, but that is my business." The faux geniality had vanished, which was fine with me. I was better prepared for his shark persona.

"Of course, I'd make it worth your while," he added.

"And I assume you'll want to be billed separately for these preview reports?"

"I'm sure we could work out a cash bonus . . . ."

"That's not how I work, Mr. Ericson. I can draw up another contract and bill you separately through your office, and of course it will be confidential. But any work I do for you will be included in my tax records."

"You know, I wouldn't have expected someone like you to be such a stickler for propriety." Ericson's face had turned magenta. He was obviously holding himself back. "Very well. Prepare the contract and fax it to this number, marked confidential." He scribbled a phone number on a napkin and pushed it toward me.

"Would you like me to pursue a different angle in this separate contract?"

"No, I want you to find the Henry girl. But I also want to make sure that neither my wife nor my daughter gets hurt." He stopped, took in my blank look, and continued. "There are some things that you might come across . . . . They're irrelevant to finding Ms. Henry, but they could be hurtful to innocent people. I don't want to go into details now. Just keep doing what you've been doing, but get it to me first."

"Do you have any information that could help move the investigation along? Anything you could tell me in confidence that you might not have wanted to say earlier?"

"That's all I can tell you, Ms. Garrett."

I excused myself, enjoying the confusion on his face when I counted out a generous tip for the man behind the bar. I walked double-time to my car, shaking myself to get rid of his presence the way a dog shakes off water. After only a few hours, I was having second, third and fourth thoughts about this case.

CHAPTER SIX

There were a half-dozen errands that needed running, but I needed a dose of reality even more. Home beckoned in all its scruffy comfort. I stepped in the door to my own twentieth-century version of Dickensian domestic bliss: greetings, complaints and joyful reunions with the animals, the place tidy or a wreck, depending on my mood or schedule, a fridge full of rotting greens and, if I was lucky, the better part of a pint of frozen yogurt.

And of course the routine assortment of messages on my answering machine. Diana Hoffman, my current flame, had returned my call during the afternoon (why hadn't she called my office, unless she preferred leaving a message to talking in person?). An urgent request to call from my friend Liam O'Meara. An invitation from Jessie to come for breakfast with her and Tate and a new neighbor: "She's a sculptor, and she's very opinionated. I think you'd like her."

Sure, Jessie. Just like the last five women you tried to fix me up with. Jessie and Tate are one of those model couples whose lives are seamlessly interwoven, and Jessie's matchmaking comes from the belief that no one could be single *and* happy. She considers it her responsibility to find the perfect match for me, with or without my participation. The sculptor neighbor might have sounded more promising if Jessie didn't push every unattached lesbian she met in my direction.

The question was, how unattached was I? I had met Diana Hoffman six months earlier in our roles of homicide detective and P.I. From the start there had been an electrical charge between us. Our first and only date, a candle-lit dinner, had begun full of promise. It ended before we got to dessert. She was called to the scene of a domestic murder. Then she'd been on leave for two months taking care of her younger step-siblings in Nashville while their father spent his last days fighting colon cancer.

For over a month, we'd been trying sporadically to set up another date. To tell the truth, she was sporadic; I was determined. One glance from those expressive eyes made me lose my composure. Her mouth betrayed her vulnerability, or I wanted to believe it did, at least for me. This might be the woman of my dreams, and I was hell-bent on finding out. I dialed her number. The line was busy.

Deciding not to decide yet about Jessie's breakfast invitation, I called Liam. No answer, but then he always screened his calls. "It's me, pick up, pick up!" The yell was in case he was at the other end of the long apartment he shared with his lover Sam. I was about to give up when he answered.

"Maggie, I need a place to stay tonight . . . ."

"Oh, honey, I'm sorry. What happened now?"

"We had The Big Talk About Monogamy yesterday. It was a disaster, and I ended up sleeping on the couch. Actually, sleep had nothing to do with my experience of last night. I writhed around on the couch until dawn."

"At which time you got up and rearranged all the furniture."

"I have to make some new friends—you know me too well."

"Want to come over and writhe around on *my* couch all night?"

"Could I?"

"Of course. You always stay here when you leave Sam forever. It's a tradition."

"Maggie!"

"I'm sorry, that was mean. But this is the third final bust-up in five months. So come think it over at Maggie's Pet Fur Emporium. You know I love having you here. Just remember how much you complained about Fearless trying to smother you the last time you slept over."

"It'll make for a nice change. Sam says I'm smothering his independence, whatever the hell that means! I'll be over in an hour."

Poor Liam. By my wholly objective reckoning, he had made all the compromises in that relationship. He had even sent his beloved wolfhound Loba to live with his parents, because Sam was allergic.

Why was true love so elusive? I could feel a "relationships suck" mood coming on: I enumerate all the sick, stale or plain-old unhappy couple formations in my friendship circle. Experience has shown that this kind of negative thinking lands me in bed with someone thrilling but truly unsuitable.

I dialed Diana's number again. This time she answered on the first ring.

"Hi, Diana, it's Maggie."

"Hi, how are you?"

"Just fine. How are you?"

"I'm fine." Well, *this* was certainly worth the wait. We talked about the craziness of our schedules for a few minutes (she won in the no-free-time category), compared notes on movies, plays and an art exhibit both of us had read about but hadn't been able to attend. Finally I took the leap.

"Diana, I want to see you again. Soon."

There was silence for a full three seconds. I reminded myself to breathe. "Um, well, that would be great. Let me get my book," she said.

"I know it's short notice, but how about tomorrow night? My friend Erroll is opening a restaurant, and he's inviting everyone he knows to pack the place. He said I could bring a guest."

"Tomorrow night is fine." Her southern vowels became more prominent in unguarded moments like this one.

"Wonderful. Shall I pick you up?"

"No, I'll come by your house. Eight o'clock all right?"

"Perfect." I had hoped for six or seven, but I'd settle.

As soon as I put down the phone, it rang again. Sylvia Ericson apologized for calling me at home, but asked me to meet her at her club for breakfast the next morning. "It's a private matter. I'd rather not discuss it on the phone."

As we negotiated a time, I marveled over the layers of intrigue that this family was bringing into my life. A daughter set on not defending herself, a father with things to hide from his wife and daughter, and now a stepmother with confidential needs. Thanks a lot for the referral, Tate.

CHAPTER SEVEN

The sounds coming from the kitchen at six o'clock the next morning reminded me of why I don't cohabit. Whatever Liam was cooking involved the banging of multiple pans. After a few seconds of silence, he stuck his head through the bedroom door.

"Didn't you get a Cuisinart for Christmas one time?" I sat open-mouthed, unable to formulate a suitably crushing retort. "I distinctly remember discussing how you could use a food processor when Debbie, or Libbie, or Cissie sent it to you." The animals sidled around Liam and into the bedroom, food on their minds.

My sister Melissa, known to the family as Missie, had indeed sent me a Cuisinart, which took up most of my counter space. After six months passed without my so much as touching it except to blow off cat hair, I had given it to the Community United Against Violence sidewalk sale. I explained this to Liam with what I considered to be extraordinary restraint. He hung his head, stuck out his lower lip, and retreated to the kitchen. I hurled a shoe at the closing door.

"Missed me! You always were a rotten pitcher, Garrett," he sing-songed through the door.

I punched my pillow and fluffed the comforter around me, pretending that there was a ghost of a chance for more sleep. The dog and cats were now shut in the room with me. Pugsley burrowed under the covers and nudged my foot with his ice-cube nose just as I was drifting off, and the cats enacted a hissing, snarling war game on the bed for my benefit.

Surrendering to the inevitable, I threw on my old chenille robe and staggered in the direction of the coffee pot. Unlike every other morning of my life, there was no automatic timer-brewed coffee. I flicked the On button. Nothing.

"What happened to the coffee?"

"Oh, it started making these wheezy noises, and I didn't know if it was supposed to be doing that, so I unplugged it."

"Aargh! It took me an hour to get the digital clock and timer set up! Well, *you* can get out the anal-retentive ten-page instruction manual and figure out how to program it again." This is what I said. In my brain a caffeine-starved demon demanded that Liam be put to the knife, now.

"I'm sorry, Maggie."

"Why didn't you ask me?"

"I didn't want to wake you."

Rather than scream accusations about Cuisinarts and what he could do with the next one he encountered, I took a shower. After I had immersed myself under running water for a few minutes I felt much better, and more tolerant. Liam served me eggs and home fries and made me coffee brewed with a filter in a colander. Life was good.

"So have you talked to Sam yet?"

"Maggie, it's not even seven o'clock—"

"Uh-huh. Have you talked to him yet?"

"Well, I did call to make sure he was up. He's been oversleep-ing lately."

"And—"

"And it was tense, but he said he didn't sleep well last night, and he missed me." I waited, knowing there was more. "Then I asked him why he didn't answer the phone at midnight, and he told me he'd been at the Jackhammer."

"Alone?"

"I don't know. He wants to be able to go out and trash around. I'm not supposed to mind. I do mind. That's why I'm here instead of in my own apartment."

"Just remember that when he starts missing you and getting all kissy purr-purr. That's when you always cave in."

"I know. Lucky thing that I have you to remind me."

I put on minimal makeup and then underwent a social-class metamorphosis via my four-year-old Norma Kamali outfit, which Liam calls my rich-hetero drag. In the space of two days I had worn my entire upper-crust repertoire for the Ericsons. I resolved to hike my rates for cases that required extensive wardrobe changes. Carefully avoiding the animals, whose hair leaps onto my clothing as if it had a life of its own, I ran to the car.

I had an appointment with Chad Osafune at the Glass Security Agency at seven thirty. The reason for this ungodly hour was that we could be finished before his boss or the other agency Neanderthals came in. Glass Security was known for muscle uninformed by intelligence. A famous rock promoter used them as extra thugs at his oversold concerts, where they stood out in their puce satin jackets with the Glass logo: a staring eyeball centered in a spyglass. Real classy stuff.

Chad met me at the elevator, beaming. No question about this guy being a morning person. Chad's invisibility in a crowd is a source of pride with him. That day he was wearing an over-sized jumpsuit with "Hercules Movers" embroidered on his chest, and his walk had taken on a weight lifter's lumbering swagger.

"Fabulous camouflage, Chad." I wasn't sure whether the punkish stiffness of his hair was part of the disguise or a bad hair day, so I avoided commenting on it.

Chad and I have run into each other on jobs a couple of times and, against conventional expectations for a straight man and a lesbian, took an immediate shine to each other. One long, boring afternoon, while we waited for a client (who ultimately stiffed both of us), we had exchanged life stories.

Chad told me about his Japanese immigrant parents' vehement opposition when he refused to enter a profession or the family business. He compounded this by becoming a cop. After two miserable years in the LAPD, he fled Los Angeles and his extended family and took a job as a P.I. for Roy Glass in San Francisco.

This sealed our friendship, since I'm a disappointment to my family too: I turned out queer, didn't graduate from college, live in Earthquake Central and make a living by sitting in my car waiting for lovers to demonstrate their infidelity, for workers on disability to flaunt their skills at skateboarding or for shoppers in Victoria's Secret to pocket a lace garter belt.

Chad is conversant in four or five languages, a major plus in this metropolitan city. He has a reputation for keeping a cool head in a crisis, and he's a highly inventive comedian, which makes him good company during those endless surveillance shifts. If I ever have enough business to take on a partner, my first call will be to Chad Osafune.

"So, Chad, when are you going to leave that sleazy bunch of losers?" My late partner and mentor, Jack Windsor, had carried on a feud for decades with Roy Glass, and I felt obliged to carry on the tradition of Glass-bashing. It occurred to me that Jack had never filled me in on the reason for the feud. Possibly he had forgotten its origin himself.

Chad recognized the ritual and tossed some abuse back in my direction. "Here I thought you'd come to your senses and decided to work for a living. I figured you were gonna ask me to help you get hired at Glass. You know I got big influence with the boss!" He laughed at his own joke and removed his steaming mug of *miso* from the microwave. It smelled tempting, but I turned down his offer of a mug. Almost three decades of Western acculturation stood in the way of soup for breakfast. Besides, it didn't go with my takeout coffee and raspberry danish.

He gave me a between-the-lines summary of his surveillance report. He and his partner had been told to watch the comings and goings at Kelly's house, which had been like monitoring an anthill. Besides the daily entrances and exits of residents, the agents had recorded multiple drug deals and a steady prostitution business, a fight between two prostitutes over a pimp, and then a beating of the loser by the pimp. The regulars at the house included at least two additional prostitutes, a half-dozen IV drug users (identified when they participated in a needle exchange that AIDS activists conducted on the block), several street people who were probably homeless for part of each month, and an almost unbelievable number of families from Mexico, Central America and a half-dozen Asian countries. But no sign of Kelly.

"Are they keeping you on at the house?"

"Two shifts. Paolo Arce and I drew the night watch. You know Paolo?"

"Yeah, I do." I knew Paolo from gay political activities, but I wasn't sure he was out to Chad. "How did Roy end up with two talented people of color? Isn't he afraid you'll overrun him and his beefy white hunks?"

"They don't know what to do with either one of us," Chad said, with a chuckle. "At the Christmas party last year, I played a joke on Mr. Glass. Everybody laughed, except Mr. Glass. He says I undermined his authority. Then Paolo has to open his big mouth and tell one of the guys he's gay. So now some of the other guys are nervous about working with him—you know how that homosexual stuff rubs off. And I'm the one who made the boss look stupid, so they're afraid to work with me . . . .

That's how Paolo and I ended up partners. It's fine with us. He promised he won't come on to me and I promised not to correct his lousy English."

"Can you tell me how the Ericsons got a copy of Kelly's journal?"

"Are you trying to get free lessons in P.I. work? Just kidding. I don't know who made the transaction, or exactly how much money passed hands, but the Ericsons have a lot of money to throw at a problem, if you know what I mean. Somebody from Missing Persons will be able to take his vacation in Tahiti this year . . . . "

"Thanks, Chad. Glass may not appreciate you and Paolo, but I do. I'll be hanging out at Kelly's place for a few days to see if anybody there knows where she went. It'll be good to know you're out there."

"We'll keep an eye on you. If you get in trouble, set the place on fire, and we'll call in an alarm."

CHAPTER EIGHT

The Barbary Club, synonymous with old San Francisco wealth and privilege, occupied the top floors of an office building on Sansome Street. Below, appointments were being made, offers tendered, mergers consummated, souls delivered to Satan. Thousands of white-collar workers were drinking coffee out of paper cups and booting up or logging on. Here on the thirty-fourth floor there was no sense of time, or of effort expended. The Barbary Club could be in another country or another century.

With exquisite hauteur, a man in Edwardian morning dress escorted me through a maze of suites to an intimate dining room. Heavy curtains hushed all noise of our passage and prevented conversations from carrying. The carpets were so deep that moving across them was like trudging through sand.

My guide seated me and fled, refusing to meet my eyes. Both of us knew I was an imposter and he didn't want to be contaminated by contact with me. I felt like a child at her first grown-up occasion and tried not to gawk. In this kind of atmosphere I get an almost overwhelming urge to sing cowboy songs, or Iggy Pop, or the *Internationale*.

Concentrate on your surroundings, Garrett. I examined our little pavilion. The decor was ostentatious to the point of self-parody. My elbow sank into the table, which was practically upholstered in multiple layers of linen. I was engulfed by deep

Victoriana.

After a few minutes Sylvia Ericson was escorted in by the same man, who bowed to her for the signal honor of this duty. Sylvia was dressed in a finely tailored grey-green suit. Her hair was pulled back severely, which oddly made her look younger and more accessible.

"Thank you so much for meeting me," she said, smiling and studying my outfit.

"No problem. Of course, I don't have much to report so far." I silently affirmed: Wearing old clothes demonstrates a sense of self-esteem. What an abundance of self-esteem I have. The affirmation wasn't working well.

A waiter appeared at her elbow. She greeted him by name and asked about his progress in applying for a creative writing grant. He marked his pad with her request for her "usual," and congratulated her on her choice. He took my order without comment.

Sylvia turned back to me. "I asked you to meet me because I need your help. This is entirely separate from the arrangement you made with us yesterday. Maggie, I want to be honest with you. I can't offer additional payment for this, but I believe I can be of considerable help to you."

"I appreciate honesty, Ms. Ericson. Could you tell me a little more about what you had in mind?"

"Please, Maggie, my name is Sylvia." The waiter brought our orders, bowed deeply and departed. Sylvia glanced wistfully at my plenteous portions of eggs and muffins, and reached for her mineral water with lime.

"I spend several months a year in San Francisco, and I have many friends here. Sometimes they need help with sensitive matters," she said, selecting a slice of her "usual" dry toast as she spoke. "My friends would respect my judgment about your qualifications."

"I always welcome referrals—"

"What I'm suggesting is more than a referral, Maggie. Although I'm not attracted to women myself, some of my friends are." Reaching across me for a fruit spread, she met my bewildered glance. "Besides being a lovely young woman, you're quite exotic—a private detective who wears vintage Kamali." She allowed her patrician nose to wrinkle slightly with the word "vintage," payback for my Eggs Florentine, perhaps.

"Sylvia—" I began.

"Yesterday I felt an immediate sense of connection with you. I don't expect us to become friends, but I hope that as women we share a certain empathy . . . ." She covered my hand with both of hers. I removed mine. Something flared in the back of her eyes, but I couldn't tell what emotion was attached to it.

She continued, "As I told you, I need a special favor from you. In return, I can help you meet a wealthy backer. As a small business owner, you can use friends with influence, to help you over slow times."

"Sorry, you seem to have mistaken me for someone else. I'm not for sale." I scooped up my bag and rose from the table. Sylvia clasped my elbow with a surprisingly strong grip.

"Don't leave," she said softly. "I apologize. I've gone about this the wrong way. I'd prefer being frank with you, anyway. Are you aware that you inspire trust? I need someone I can trust."

I sat back down, my outrage overtaken by my curiosity. "Apology accepted," I said. "But please, tell me what you think I can do besides what we've already discussed." After the meeting with Howard Ericson, I had a pretty good idea of what she was about to propose. Were the Ericsons' whole lives spent deceiving each other?

"You must have wondered why Moira refuses our help," Sylvia said. "She won't reconcile with Howard as long as he's with me. Moira hates me, far more I'm sure than she could ever admit, especially to herself. But I can see it, and, of course, so can her father. For as long as Moira is in trouble, she exercises power over Howard. She can still make him feel guilty for marrying me, for not being with Ellen, Moira's mother, when she died, and for not spending the rest of his life mourning Ellen."

"I'm sorry. It must be very difficult for you. But how can I help?"

"The favor I need from you relates to my relationship with my husband. I want you to continue your investigation, as we arranged yesterday. But, if you uncover anything that might . . . compromise my reputation, you will bring it to me, and to no one else."

"Does this relate to Kelly being missing?"

For the first time Sylvia Ericson seemed unsure and uncomfortable. "I assure you that it does not bear on what transpired between Kelly Henry and Moira."

"But you and Kelly know each other?"

"She might believe that she knows me, but I assure you, she doesn't!" Sylvia's face contorted with emotion for a half-second. Then, her self-control restored, she smiled as if we were discussing the fresh flowers on our table.

"Kelly Henry's involvement with Moira is the only thing that matters," she said. "I want you to find out what's happened to Ms. Henry. The only difference is that I need to know where she is before you tell Howard or Summers."

"You obviously know more about Kelly than you told me earlier. Why not tell me the rest, so I can take care of this for you as quickly as possible?"

"I'm sorry, I can't tell you any more. Please don't press me," she said with finality.

"If I can help you within the boundaries of our contract, I will. However, I'll decline your offer to find me a lover!" My voice rose in pitch. I made myself smile and take a deep breath.

"I certainly had no plans to force anyone on you," she said lightly. "There is, of course, the business I could send your way."

"As I told you, I appreciate new business. Ninety percent of my business is referrals. Of course I'll be delighted to meet any of your friends as clients. But I'm rather private about my personal life. I'd rather keep stumbling along on my own in my relationships."

"You'll find that everything looks different as you get older, Maggie." She took another sip of her mineral water.

"I have a proposal for you," I said. "I'll give you any information I find twelve hours before I report it to Summers, and I'll hold back any embarrassing details about you. In return, you'll give me any leads you have on how to find Kelly." She was quiet for a long time. Then she blew out her breath as if she were exhaling smoke.

"There's very little that I can add to what you know about Kelly Henry. What I couldn't say when we met before is . . . I believe something has happened to her. She didn't just run off."

"Why do you say that?"

Sylvia turned so that her beautiful eyes stared straight into mine.

We were only inches apart. "There was a meeting that she wouldn't have missed. It was extremely important to her."

"Was the meeting with you?"

"Forgive me if I'm not prepared to confide in you yet, Maggie. These things take time." The waiter brought her a heavy leather folder with our bill. She dashed off her signature and began to gather her possessions. We were done.

"Sylvia, how should I contact you?"

"You can leave messages for me at this number." She wrote a local phone number on a slip of paper and handed it to me. Two polished blondes, wearing thousands of dollars worth of understated clothing, approached us. Sylvia took a deep breath, and her expression changed to impersonal friendliness. The three women made casual, superficial conversation. She didn't introduce me, and they didn't ask. I ate my eggs.

When they had gone, Sylvia held onto the tone she had assumed with them. "Let's meet here at the club again on Sunday and you can fill me in on everything. Howard has to go back to Phoenix for the weekend and I'll be on my own. Sunday brunch here is spectacular. The weather has been lovely—we can sit on the terrace. Everyone throws off her diet for a day, although you obviously don't need to worry about that. It's like an English garden party. Wear a hat if you have one. In the meantime, expect a call from an old friend of mine who needs help from someone like you . . . ."

Sylvia joined the women she had spoken to earlier. She said something and they all laughed. I caught them giving me surreptitious looks as I trudged through the heavy carpeting toward the exit.

I stopped in the Women's Room on my way out. It was the full-service model, complete with an elderly attendant. She nodded a greeting and eyed me curiously. As I was closing the door of the stall, two women came into the restroom, speaking what I thought might be Vietnamese. One of them switched to English to joke with the attendant.

"Estrella, I see your favorite lady here today!"

"Who you mean? I've got so many, many!"

"Mrs. Powers."

"That one! She richest lady here, and she *never* tips. But, 'Estrella,' she say, 'get me this and get me that,' and always she needs it right now!"

"Never tip, hah! Two weeks ago I do a full set of nails, big emergency. But this lady so particular—every nail, she tells me do it over. Takes me two hours. So I tell her the cost is forty dollars. *She* says I take too long, and the shape not right, so she only pay the price for fill-ins. And, no tip!"

The attendant snorted in disgust. "What did you do?"

"What can you do? I say thank you Mrs. and I take her twenty-five dollars. But I never will do her again, no!"

A club member entered and spoke to the attendant. The other women left with brief good-byes.

I rearranged my expensive drag over my hips and left the stall to wash my hands under Estrella's watchful eyes and accept the towel she offered. On my way out I sheepishly fished a dollar out of my purse for her.

This case continued to amaze me. Just when I thought it couldn't get more complicated, a new facet appeared. Both of the Ericsons wanted to be the first to receive any news about the case, which presented an interesting question of ethics, not to mention logistics. I didn't buy Sylvia's story about wanting to help Moira so that her stepdaughter would no longer command so much of Howard's attention. On the other hand, Howard had come across as the reluctant partner in the transaction, so Sylvia must be the moving force here. The Sylvia-Kelly angle was tantalizing. How they had known one another, and what was the connection to Moira?

CHAPTER NINE

The building lobby featured a bank of enclosed pay phones. I slid into the only vacant one just inches ahead of a businessman who had been slowed down by his briefcase and laptop. He stood and glared his outrage for a few seconds while I dialed my office number. Ricardo had left a rambling rundown on his efforts to track Kelly Henry, with no results so far. Jessie's message was a reminder of her invitation to breakfast with the sculptor who was perfect for me, perhaps my machine was broken—otherwise, surely I would have called her back? Someone from the Titan Trust Company notified me that, based on my references and experience, I'd made it to the final round for becoming their local fraud investigator, and they would be in touch. An influential former client had helped get my name onto a short list for this contract. The hours of filling out Titan's forms and convincing other clients to vouch for me might pay off.

For a few minutes I reveled in imagining what it would mean to have an ongoing corporate client. Titan wouldn't care whether I was gay or straight, butch or femme. Titan would never call and demand that I meet it for breakfast. Most importantly, Titan would cut checks with machine-like regularity.

"Never forget who you are, Maggie." My mentor Jack Windsor's voice intruded. "They're on the other side, Maggie, the big companies, the government, the rich bastards."

Jack's business consisted of obtaining evidence of marital infidelity and providing legwork for a seedy assortment of defense and personal injury attorneys. He refused to take "bureaucrat" jobs, like the one with Titan. My suggestion that a bread-and-butter arrangement might make life easier had led to our biggest fight.

"But Jack," I said now, "if I don't take on one of these outfits as a regular client, I could end up back at a corporate law firm, researching toxic torts." There was no longer anyone to fight with me about it. Few would even criticize such a move. I was only responsible to myself, my creditors and the bourbon-scented ghost of Jack Windsor.

The trainer at my gym promises me that staying limber in my twenties will help stave off arthritis in decades to come. The benefit at the moment is that I can change my clothes in the car. Back in my real-life outfit of leggings, T-shirt and a shocking pink sweater knit by Great-Aunt Ellen, I drove to Kelly's house.

This part of the Mission District has not seen so much as a whiff of gentrification. Thousands of immigrants, mostly from Central America and Southeast Asia, are packed into small apartments, and poor people of a dozen races and nationalities are warehoused in badly built projects. Liquor stores are the only thriving retail stores on many blocks, and prostitution and drug dealing thrive regardless of how many cops walk the streets. I parked my car next to a gas station and hoped the windows would be intact when I returned.

The house where Kelly had lived was on Capp Street. It must have been built as a boarding house a hundred years ago. Whatever use had been made of it in the intervening decades, it was once again, unofficially, a boarding house. Only one doorbell dangled from frayed wires, and no names were listed on the rusty mailbox next to it. The front door was ajar, so I walked in. All of the rooms off the filthy hall were fastened with padlocks.

A tired-looking Asian woman weighted down with grocery bags of produce hurried through the doorway, eyed me cautiously and ran up the stairs. A half-starved cat slid inside but withdrew swiftly when she saw me. A man whose face was concealed by tawny dreadlocks staggered in, dragging a train of garbage bags full of bottles. I saw a bit of reddish-brown skin when he peered at me over his shoulder.

"Excuse me, I heard there was a room for rent here. Can you tell me who to see about it?" The man grunted in reply and went back outside for another bag of stuff.

"You got any money?" The voice came from behind me.

"Not with me, but I'll have it this afternoon. I'm Maggie," I said to the long-haired man standing in the doorway closest to the entrance.

"Al here. How'd you find out about the room?" When he grinned, he showed blackened stumps instead of teeth. Otherwise he looked like a lot of men who had never left the sixties.

"On the street. Is there a room?"

"Might be. Where you from?"

"From here in the city, but I had some relationship problems." The last phrase rang false, but "girlfriend" was asking for trouble, and I couldn't get "boyfriend" to come out of my mouth. "I need a place to stay right away."

"Police after you? Got an old man with a gun looking for you?"

"No and no. It was just time to get out of there, and I heard this place was cool." I tried to remember how my Uncle Walt, a Green Beret turned pothead, would talk. He was about the same era as this man.

"Want to see the room?"

"Sure." I followed him up two flights of stairs that stank of urine and vomit. "My" room was near the stairway.

"This is it," he said, turning a key in the heavy padlock on the door. It was a 10 x 12 room with a small closet. A battered double bed took up most of its floor space. The other furniture consisted of what we called a chest of drawers back in Iowa, a nightstand, a straight chair and a wobbly table large enough to seat one diner. It smelled strongly of stale cigarette smoke, Lysol, and something else I couldn't identify.

"Am I the only one who'd have a key?"

"Just you and me, and I don't go nowhere I'm not asked." His bloodshot eyes glittered, and he showed those stubs of teeth again. "That's some sweater. I can still see that color when I shut my eyes." He demonstrated closing his eyes.

"Who lives next door?"

"Girl who used to stay in that one has gone missing," he jerked his head toward the door on the left. "So the cops made me lock up her room, leave everything in it. Then they go away and forget about it. Is that fucked up, or what? I can't rent it, but she's not paying." He went to another reality, perhaps another solar system, for a minute. His eyes lost their focus. Was he thinking about Kelly, or the money he was losing? Was he thinking? A shiver passed through him and he came back.

"Down that end of the hall I got a whole nest of some kind of Orientals. This place is a regular United Nations. I got a Mexican witch on the second floor—watch out for her, she's got the evil eye. Other side of you is another girl, Lisa. She's a little younger than you. She's got a lot of men friends coming around. Hah! That's a good one. They come and they go." He laughed loudly at his pun, showing even more of the stubs.

"How much?"

"It costs extra because it's furnished."

"That's okay, I don't have any furniture. How much is it?"

"Three twenty-five a month, or ninety a week, or fifteen dollars a night."

"How about a hundred fifty for two weeks, paid in advance?"

He shut his eyes to do the math.

"You've got a good head for numbers, Maggie, is it? Never met a pretty girl could do arithmetic! Sure, get it to me this afternoon, you can move in tonight. When you bring me the money, I'll turn you on to some killer weed a friend of mine from Humboldt County grows."

"Oh, wow, thanks, but I had to give up grass. I've got asthma. I'll see you this afternoon, though."

CHAPTER TEN

June 16. She has a beautiful office full of dolls and toys. I wish I could stay there all the time. Moira said I have special problems, and that it's incredibly lucky that I came to her, because she's one of the only therapists in the whole country that could help me.

June 26. Last night I had a dream about her and me. She always has me tell her my dreams, and sometimes I act them out. She wanted to hear everything about this one. I was so embarrassed. She said it was a good sign that I was having a sexual dream about somebody safe, who would never hurt me.

July 10. She told me that if I want to get well faster, we can do a special kind of therapy. It will take a lot of work and I'll need extra sessions. She said it's controversial, and people always are afraid of what's new. But she says it's going to be written up in books some-day. She hugged me and said, men took away your body but I'm going to give it back to you.

I get the willies when I hear about therapy styles that are more, well, intrusive than that of my own solemn butch therapist, who stayed in her chair, didn't profess to have special powers, and never touched me except to shake hands at the end of our last session. I know, what works for one person won't necessarily be right for another. I just have a hard time with anyone who sets herself up as having a lock on repairing the human psyche.

The more I read of Kelly's journal, the more my sympathies grew for this lonely young woman in a strange city, trusting completely in a therapist who claimed to have all the answers. But the therapist wanted to get her client out of her clothes, and charge her for it, to boot. A gnawing apprehension was growing in me that I was working for the wrong side, and that I would end up 1) not getting paid, 2) sued for breach of contract, 3) put in jail for whacking my new "landlord" Al, my client Howard Ericson or my new boss at Harmony Foods, Jerry Reardon.

Speaking of Alternative Retail, I was late for my first shift at the health food store. I could blame it on a streetcar breakdown coming from school. The notoriously unreliable MUNI makes a reliable scapegoat, since it is subject to mysterious breakdowns that trap its passengers underground until the problem is, just as mysteriously, resolved.

Although there were few customers in the store, it was humming with activity. Employees gossiped and joked as they restocked shelves. Representatives from three bakeries jostled amicably as they lined up loaves in their allocated shelf spaces. One of the male cashiers I remembered from the day before waved hello.

Jerry gestured me over to where he was standing. I started to apologize for being late, but he brushed it aside. He guided me to the back of the store, his hand possessively on my back. One woman employee signaled to another with the in-and-out gesture of fist and forefinger as they watched Jerry and me pass. Surely she wasn't suggesting that I'd have sex with Jerry? A third woman caught my eye and blushed deep red. This place was in serious need of a sexual harassment workshop.

"You can keep your things here," he said, pointing to a rack of coats and bags. I slid out of my jacket before he could "help" me.

Jerry put me to work inventorying the gourmet foods section, located near his office. The disadvantage of this was that he could keep an eye on me. The upside was that I could hear his phone calls. He was having problems with his bank, or rather, they had problems with him. Twice he answered the phone in a disguised voice and told the caller that Mr. Reardon wasn't in. Finally he took a call and shut the door of the office. I knelt to pick up inventory cards I had "accidentally" dropped and put my head against the door, but I couldn't make out any words.

Time for a reconnaissance break. I approached the woman who had made the obscene gesture when she saw Jerry and me together.

"Hi, I'm Maggie Garrett. I'm interning here for school."

"Hey, Maggie. I'm Cecelia. We heard you were coming this morning. Watch out for Jerry, especially if he says he wants to make you his personal assistant . . . ."

"Yeah, I noticed he's really interested in my career development," I said, laughing. "Thanks for the tip!"

Cecelia was probably in her late thirties. She must have been Hollywood-beautiful once, and she was still trying to look the way she did then. Her clothes were too bright and too revealing, her makeup garish. Like a parrot in a flock of pigeons, she stuck out among the other all-cotton, no-makeup employees and customers.

I wandered to the front of the store. A stick-thin, grey-faced man introduced himself as Daryl, the vitamin buyer and head cashier. I acted duly impressed with his title and told him my intern story, adding that a woman I knew had told me about the store. Her name was Kelly—did he know her?

"Yeah, she worked here for a few months, but she didn't talk much. I never knew her."

"So she's not here anymore? That's too bad."

"Maybe for you," he growled, and turned away. I returned to counting jars of sun-dried tomatoes, flavored vinegars and squeeze-tubes of pesto.

At noon, Jerry came up behind me and gave me a pat on the rear. "How about some lunch? I'll buy."

"Oh, thanks, but I'm going to have to leave by two o'clock. I don't have time for a lunch break."

"You've got to eat, honey. Don't want you to shrink away on us." His hand followed the curve of my buttock downward.

"Well, thanks. I'll get my jacket." I stepped aside so abruptly that Jerry almost lost his balance.

"We can stay right here. There's a whole store full of food. That way we can get to know each other."

My fantasies of smacking him silly with frozen tofu weenies were interrupted by the arrival of two State Health Department officials for an unscheduled inspection. I faded away as Jerry drew them hastily into his office.

Daryl ushered out the few straggler customers and declared an early lunch break for all but two of the employees. While Jerry schmoozed with the bureaucrats, Daryl directed his remaining cadre to clean up or remove violations, one eye on the closed door of Jerry's office. The rest of us stampeded for the store entrance.

On the sidewalk out front, several of the women employees were comparing notes about where to eat. Cecelia leaned in my direction. "Guess you'll have to put off 'getting to know each other,'" she cackled.

"I never really appreciated the Health Department before," I said, grinning. "Makes me proud to be a taxpayer." I turned to the women. "May I buy you lunch? I promise to keep *my* hands to myself, and I'd love to get the low-down on this place."

"Let's go to that Japanese place," chirped a Rubens blonde with dimples everywhere, who introduced herself as Patty.

"It's not cheap," warned Cecelia.

"I can swing it," I replied. "Let's get out of here before we get called to duty!"

CHAPTER ELEVEN

The Nature's Harmony women were making serious headway on their sushi combination plates when I dropped my bomb.

"I'm a private investigator." They stopped chewing and stared. "I've been hired to find a woman who's been missing for a couple of weeks. She worked at the store. What can you tell me about Kelly Henry?" That ended the silence. Kelly's name provoked an outpouring of dislike and scorn.

"That slut." "Snotty bitch." "I was glad to see the last of her."

My shock on hearing this must have been visible. It was hard to tell who was more surprised. They were amazed that anyone would care what happened to Kelly. I knew her only as the frail victim described in her journal. She might be absurdly gullible and easily led, but a "snotty bitch"?

"Sounds like she isn't missed around here," I said, trying to regain my bearings. "What did she do that made you all dislike her so much?"

"For one thing," said Cecelia, who had resumed eating, "she was doing it with Jerry, right there in his office, which he already wanted us to think was a part of our job description. Now that she's gone, he's started putting the moves on other women."

Pretty Leslie, who had said nothing since we introduced ourselves, froze at these words. Of the four, she was by far the least assertive, and Jerry might take her shyness for acceptance. She picked up her tea with a shaking hand and our eyes met. She set down the cup and swung her long brown hair forward. It formed a curtain along the side of her face. She might as well be wearing a veil.

"Yeah, Kelly was Jerry's little pet," said Annette, a pallid, slouching woman with a nasal voice. She was dressed in variegated shades of ivory to taupe. "Plus, she spied on us. Every time you looked over your shoulder, there she was."

"Spying?"

"She was always writing things down, and turning up right behind you without making any noise," Cecelia said. "We thought for awhile she was from the Health Department, or OSHA or something. But when she and Jerry got so friendly, we figured she was spying for *him*."

Patty nodded her agreement vehemently but didn't interrupt the progress of food to her mouth.

"Did anyone ever ask her about it?" I asked.

"Cecelia did, of course," Patty said, and gave Cecelia a friendly nudge. "Kelly told her to mind her own business."

"I heard the police came to the store when she disappeared. Did they talk to any of you?" Their heads swiveled around to see the others' responses, as curious as me about the answers. Each answered no.

"The only reason I knew the cops had been around was because GT, the produce guy, said they'd scared the bejeebees out of old Jerry," Annette said thoughtfully. "Jerry's got so many scams going, I bet he couldn't even figure out what lie to tell!"

"What happened when Kelly didn't show up at work? Was Jerry upset?"

"He put on a show like he was mad," said Cecelia, "but I think he was relieved. Business is down. I figured he'd been planning to lay somebody off, and now he won't have to."

"But you know," Patty interrupted, thinking aloud, "the two

of them hadn't been so friendly right before she left. Maybe she kicked him out of bed." She giggled, looking at the others for validation. Seeing none, she shrugged and dove back into her food.

I was keeping an eye on Leslie. She kept poking at a morsel of raw tuna with her chopstick. Most of her food remained on her plate.

"Anything else you could tell me about the last few days Kelly was here?" I figured Cecelia would have something more to say, if only to get in the last word, and she did.

"Well, the last day she worked, she and Jerry had a long session in his office. I remember telling GT that Jerry might not have enough energy to sign our paychecks after their nooner. But then Jerry was in a crappy mood when he came out later."

"Can you remember if Kelly acted any different than usual, that last day?"

"She was the happiest I ever saw her, the icy little bitch!" Cecelia was stretching across the table with her chopsticks to pluck bits of food from the others' plates.

"Leslie, how about you?" I turned to her and she shrank back into the seat upholstery.

"No," she said, with a tremor in her voice. "I . . . I don't remember."

"You said Jerry had a scary expression on his face when he talked about Kelly, don't you remember?" Cecelia prodded.

"No, I don't remember. I have to go back. Thanks for lunch." Leslie gathered up her bag and fled.

"That Leslie is a piece of work," Patty said, as she scavenged the remaining food on Leslie's plate. "Jerry's been working on her, and she's so scared, she's gonna faint dead away when he finally makes his move on her."

"Yeah, she'd just lie there and hyperventilate," Cecelia said, grinning. "Me, I'd know just the spot to kick him . . . ."

"Haven't any of you ever heard that sexual harassment is illegal?" Hearing this discussion made me so angry that I was almost sputtering. "You could nail Jerry for this!"

"And be unemployed heroes? This isn't some big company, where you can sue 'em, make a pile of money and they have to let you keep working. Finding a part-time job is murder. I'm working on my master's degree and I can't stand driving cab anymore." Cecelia had a point. It was easy for me to talk brave. I'd be long gone when the ugly fallout of reporting Jerry landed on his employees.

"Did Kelly ever tell you about being in therapy?"

"I told you she was nuts!" Patty hooted.

"Patty!" Annette turned a scandalized face to her friend. Patty stuck out her tongue and laughed louder.

"Therapy—Maggie, you really don't get it!" Cecelia drained her tea and continued. "Kelly never talked to us. Not hello, goodbye or watch out, that box is gonna fall on you. The only ones she talked to were Jerry and GT."

"Do you think GT would talk to me?"

"Sure. He's even more of a horny toad than Jerry. Just wear something tight."

"Can you keep quiet about why I'm actually here?"

"It's gonna bust Jerry's ego wide open when he finds out you're not here to get some of his action, so count me in," laughed Patty.

"Let us know if you're gonna bust his balls, so we can get front-row seats," Cecelia added.

When we got back to the store, Jerry was still following the inspectors around, trying to distract them. They checked items on their clipboards and brushed away his jokes as well as his explanations and excuses.

I sidled over to GT, stuck out my unimpressive chest, and asked the first question that popped into my head. "Will the inspectors check on whether all this food is organic?"

He chuckled at my silly female question. "No, they look for mice, cockroaches, that kind of thing. There's a separate state organic produce organization that certifies our produce." His eyes zeroed in on my breasts, and thereafter he addressed his comments to them. "You're a student?"

"Yeah. I love to learn new things." I thought of one of the bimbo characters on TV and became her.

"Wanta come see the produce department?"

"Oh, yes." He demonstrated the sprayer he used on the greens, and interspersed his comments on hydrating lettuces with sexual innuendo about wetness. His own hose, by his telling, kept throngs of women wet and wanting more.

"A friend of mine used to work here," I said. "When she told me about the store, she mostly talked about you."

"Yeah, who's that?" He was trying to herd me toward a side room. I bent to re-tie my shoelace as a delaying tactic.

"Kelly Henry."

"No kidding, Kelly said that?" He stepped away from me a little, taking that in. "I didn't know Kelly had any friends. Anyway, she hasn't been around lately."

"Do you know how to reach her? I owe her some money, and I can finally pay her back."

"Seemed like a lot of people owed Kelly. I wouldn't worry about it." He moved closer again. "How about tonight?"

"Thanks, but I've already got a date. Why did you say I shouldn't worry about paying Kelly? Did she inherit or something? Should I hit her up for a bigger loan?"

"Forget Kelly, that girl can take care of herself. About tonight, cancel that other guy. Tell him something bigger came up. I've got a feeling about you and me."

"Another time." Another lifetime.

I never simply walked out of this store. It was always headlong flight. On the way back to my car I promised myself that when the case was over I'd come back and kick butt. Or better, teach the female employees the anti-mugging techniques Jessie made me study when I first came to San Francisco.

This was such a gratifying scenario that it took me a couple of minutes to spot the car tailing me at a discreet distance. I doubted that Robert Summers was still checking on my credentials. Maybe Howard Ericson had decided I wasn't up to the job and told the Glass Agency guys to keep track of me. Hell, for that matter, maybe Titan Trust Company was having me checked out before they signed me on.

Out of what my dad would call pure cussedness, I pulled into the right-turn lane at the last second, mightily angering the drivers behind me, who then were not disposed to let my pursuers cut in to make the same turn. By the time they did negotiate it, I had sped down an alley and reversed direction. Even though I wasn't going to the Secret Meeting Place, I didn't like being tailed, and pride demanded that I out-smart and out-drive those guys.

As I cruised for a broken meter or other semi-legal free place to park near the Symphony telemarketing office, Jack Windsor's mournful voice ragged on me for letting my temper affect business again: "Why'dya have to take everything so personal? Those poor schmucks were just doing what they get paid to do." I turned the radio up loud.

CHAPTER TWELVE

The telemarketing operation for the Western Symphony was on the second floor of a former textile factory. The bottom floor had been converted to chic restaurants for the after-the-Opera crowd. Its exposed red brick provided that special cachet of authenticity. The upstairs was even more authentic: the machinery had been moved out, desks brought in. From nineteenth- to twentieth-century sweatshop in one day.

The manager had a swank glass-enclosed office off the stairway. She had someone in her office, probably another job-seeker. I meandered down the hall to snoop around.

A cacophony of voices hit me before I reached the huge main room. Its bare walls bounced back and amplified the voices of dozens of telemarketers. Few people would stay here long, and there was no time to lose in finding anyone who had known Kelly. But how was I going to engage them in conversation long enough to get the information I needed? I suppressed a mad impulse to climb on top of a desk and yell: "Did anybody here know Kelly?"

Several callers were gesturing to the air as they described the magnificence of the symphony season to come. Some were serious, some joked with the person on the other end of the phone as if they were old friends. A few were reading a canned presentation syllable for syllable. At one end of the room was a chalkboard honor roll for high sales. It was covered with exclamation marks: "Afternoon(!) Shift—Laurie Zedom, $2,000! GREEEAT going Laurie!"

I had brought along a made-up résumé in case the manager wanted it, but she'd sounded enthusiastic when we talked on the phone, so I was expecting to be hired. Telemarketing and temping are what you do after you strike out elsewhere. Mostly I've met victims of downsizing and women who are suddenly heads-of-household in the agencies, but there are some truly peculiar characters as well. If you don't act out during the interview, you get placed. If you're competent, you get called back. If you're white, speak unaccented English and dress in a way that won't embarrass your supervisor, you get royal treatment.

"Are you Maggie?" someone shouted in my ear, and I came back to reality with a jolt.

"Yes. You must be Roxane. How do you stand the noise?"

"I try to think of it as the sound of money being made, with no added burden on the ecology. And in support of the arts! Come back to my office. It's a little bit quieter."

Roxane embodied that dying institution, the highly competent, nonthreatening career woman. She was wearing an honest-to-God navy coat dress with a white pilgrim collar, smiling through the routine of nonstop interviews for a high-turnover job. I bet some higher-up guy got credit for everything she did. Too much to glean from one interchange? Not after temping at big-time law firms for years. After they die, the likes of Roxane are interred in the sustaining walls of the buildings, which otherwise would crumble without the women's living presence.

I signed up for the afternoon shift, the same one Kelly had worked. Roxane asked who had referred me, and I gave Kelly's name. Roxane's only comment was that it was too bad Kelly didn't work here anymore. She couldn't collect the referral bonus.

"Well, if Kelly was good at this, I guess I can do it, too. *Was* she good at it?"

"She made some spectacular sales. If she had stayed, I think Kelly could've been one of our all-time top sellers," Roxane replied, gently but firmly ending this discussion.

After the paperwork was completed, I asked Roxane if I could stay awhile and observe her most experienced callers. She blinked several times and said she would see what she could do. Requests for unpaid training must be rare. She led me over to a slight, red-cheeked woman in an over-sized Dolly Parton wig.

"This is our star, Estelle. She's the only telemarketer who has a permanent calling station here. Estelle, this is Maggie. She wants to listen in for a bit. Do you mind?" Although Estelle wasn't eager to share her techniques, she wanted to please Roxane. She was minimally friendly in Roxane's presence, but dropped all pretense as soon as the manager was out of earshot.

"What do you really want?" Her gaze was as penetrating as it was hostile.

"Roxane told you, I want to see how it's done by a pro."

"Don't waste my time. Roxane's a nice lady, but I'm not."

"Okay, I'm looking for someone who used to work here, Kelly Henry. Did you know her?"

"I don't know anybody here. But if it's who I'm thinking of, she was a smoker. Go talk to the other nicotine hounds. They all hang out at the front door on their breaks." She paused to re-adjust her headset on her wig. "I can't talk anymore. I've got two kids in parochial school and I need to make at least three more sales today." She turned her back and dialed.

Was Kelly a smoker? Nobody else had mentioned it. The telemarketers who smoked would stay close by on their breaks, and with the comradery of fellow outcasts they'd strike up conversations. It was worth a try.

I went outside. Next to the front door a just-out-of-high-school and drop-dead-cool girl with matte black hair was applying a new coat of dark lipstick. Her cigarette dangled from the hand holding the mirror. A blue and red dragon tattoo wound across her cheek, its tail wrapping around her throat. This one wasn't destined for a job in the Financial District, unless it was as a bike messenger.

"Hi, could I buy a cigarette from you? I'm desperate."

She gave me a semi-hostile look but produced a pack. "That's okay, I'm always bumming myself."

"Thanks. I'm Maggie, this is my first day." She didn't respond, except to frown more deeply. "Do you know a girl named Kelly? She's the one who told me about this place, but I haven't seen her."

"I don't know many people's names." She started to move away. I moved with her.

"Kelly smokes too, that's why I thought you might have talked to her. All-American type, long, wavy light brown hair, wears it tied back in a rubber band."

"Oh, sure. The one in therapy. *That* was a scary number." She blew a series of perfect Os and studied them critically.

"She talked to you about her therapist?"

"Yeah, she was balling her. Or I guess when it's dykes that's not how you say it. Can you imagine paying somebody fifty bucks an hour to let them fuck you?"

"No, that's why I want to find Kelly. Nobody should get abused like that."

"You from the police?"

"No. Why do you think Kelly would tell you but not go to the police, or somebody else who could protect her?"

"It's not like she was complaining about her shrink when she told me. The stupid cow thought the shrink was doing her a favor! What she talked about was how to get more money to pay this wonderful person." I liked her much better now that she had dropped the fake *ennui*.

"I'm going to level with you—Kelly is missing. No one has seen her for two weeks. Did she ever say she was afraid of anybody?"

"No, we never got close or anything. Like I said, she talked about her therapist and did I know how she could get more money to give her therapist. It was like talking to a doper. Same thing. A fix is a fix." She put out her half-smoked cigarette by stabbing it into the wall, recomposed her face into its jaded mask and turned to leave.

"Wait! Just one other thing—Was there anyone else she talked to here?"

"There's a gay guy who works off and on. I think his name is Patrick," she said over her shoulder. "I saw them talking sometimes. He's not here today. He's real thin and he's got purple sores. . . I think he's got AIDS."

"Thanks, uh—" She never had given me her name.

"Any time." She gave me the merest suggestion of a smile and went back inside.

CHAPTER THIRTEEN

July 14. We started in on the dream I had about her again. She said it came out of my dream-self, and I should take responsibility for what my dream-self wanted. She told me it was important for us to act out everything from the dream. I said we were just holding each other in it, but she said I told her last week that we were kissing, too. I said I didn't think I could kiss her. She told me I wasn't taking my treatment seriously and made me go home.

July 21. She wasn't at her office when I got there, just a note on her door. It said she needed to think about whether I was willing to work with her on getting well. I sat on the floor outside her door for a long time, then I went home. I'm so afraid she'll stop seeing me.

July 28. Today she let me come back. She said my problems started when I was little, so we had to go back to when I was a baby. She held me on her lap and told me to pretend I was her *little girl. She opened up her blouse and told me that I could suck her nipples, so I could experience being her baby. I couldn't do it. She said that made her sad. I sat in her lap and cried.*

August 2. She says I'm getting worse and I need to come see her three times a week. I'm almost out of money. She said if I can't pay, we'll talk about what to do next. She's right, I am worse. Now I only feel safe in her office.

August 4. She had me take off almost all my clothes and stand in front of the mirror. She told me to say what was beautiful and sexy about my body. I didn't feel comfortable standing there in my bra and panties while she watched me. She said we had to keep doing this part of the treatment until I was comfortable with my body.

I threw the journal pages onto the counter top. The spoon from my latte clattered to the floor, startling the other customers in the Castro Street Spinelli's. They rolled their eyes at each other and returned their attention to their newspapers, or to cruising the parade of men outside through the open window.

Every time I read a page of Kelly's diary, my blood boiled. If her therapist wasn't arrested on the spot, she should at least be exposed and discredited. And I was working for this vampire's family. At least I wasn't expected to participate in her defense. Finding Kelly was growing more important to me all the time. The more I read or learned about her, the more the possibility of her having committed suicide grew in my mind. If she was still in the area, and alive, she would need friends to support her. The Ericsons' money might end up helping to bring their vicious daughter to justice. I drained the last of my coffee and strode out the door, wishing I still smoked.

I crossed two streets against the lights, in traditional Castro fashion, to Cliff's, a combination hardware, stationery, toy and costume store (it was getting on for Halloween, and the aisle with the wigs was already crowded). To make sure my Capp Street "landlord" Al didn't make an uninvited visit, I bought the heaviest padlock they had to offer—probably the only one in recent memory purchased to secure a door. It had a nice heft to it. I indulged in visualizing my brass padlock connecting with several chins on my way back to the office.

Ricardo was waiting when I arrived. "Hi, boss! I found Kelly Henry." He saw my face light up and hurried on. "It's bad news, though. Kelly Henry—the real one—died when she was two years old, back in 1971."

I slumped into a chair next to his desk and let his words sink in. Everything I thought I knew about the case had been turned sideways.

"Kelly" had used an old trick for changing your identity: read back issues of newspapers on microfilm at your local library for the obituaries of babies and toddlers born about the same time you were, obtain a copy of the death certificate, and present that to get the birth certificate. From the birth certificate an entire set of ID could be built, though it was much harder these days. Whoever this woman was, she must be smart to take on the persona of a dead child in our computer-data society.

"Maggie, you okay?" Ricardo asked worriedly.

"Yeah, I just have to get used to being flat-out wrong sometimes. But you did terrific work. The cops never got that far."

"Now what do we do?"

"We still have to find her, whatever her name is. I'll let you know what's next as soon as I figure it out." I looked at my watch. This was about the time Ricardo should be getting out of class. "By the way, how long have you been here?"

He groaned. "You know, Maggie, it'll be a real waste if you don't have kids. You got that mother tone *down!*"

"Yeah, well, I also know about diversionary tactics. Did you skip class again?"

"Not exactly. I got this idea about Kelly in biology class this morning, so I thought I'd come here and give it a few minutes during lunch period. But, you know how it goes when you get your face in the screen . . . ."

"Tell that to your principal—and your mother!" This wasn't the first time Ricardo had lost track of time following a hot lead.

I envisioned myself trying to explain to Alicia how her promising, college-bound son had become a dropout while in my employ.

"I only missed one class and study hall. I'm leaving, if it's all right with you." His feet were already in motion.

"Yeah, call it a day. Like I said, you did good." I shuffled absently through a stack of bills.

"Chill, Maggie, something always turns up," Ricardo assured me. "I've got faith in you: You'll con somebody into telling you what we need to know, like you always do."

"Thanks . . . I think."

After Ricardo left I sat and stared at the wall for awhile, assimilating the news that "Kelly Henry" had invented herself, and wondering how this affected the investigation. Did her false identity also mean that the story of abuse in her journal was false? And how did this fit in with her odd behavior at Nature's Harmony Foods? The questions kept piling up, with no answers in sight.

There was no reason for me to stick around the office. It was time to go to the Capp Street house. The tenants there might be able to give me some answers, or at least good leads, about Kelly. (Well, what else was I going to call her?) The Glass Agency had restricted Chad and Paolo to watching the exterior of the house. The cops would have interviewed anyone they could find in the house about Kelly, but I was sure they had learned nothing useful. I was also sure there had been talk among the tenants afterward, and gossip about what had happened to Kelly. I'd just have to con them, to use Ricardo's phrase, into confiding in me.

I parked a couple of blocks from the house and hauled a large box of clothing and bedding into the room. It was all old stuff that could be pitched if it couldn't be cleaned. I made up the bed, and started to put my clothes in the small dresser. Pulling out a couple of drawers convinced me to leave everything in the box. Did all the rooms smell this bad? Was it decades of unwashed bodies, dead rats (or something else) in the walls? I abandoned that line of questioning as counterproductive and likely to lead to dreams of Jeffrey Dahmer. Most of a can of room spray later (the one whose ads claimed it could make any room smell like a field of flowers), the place still reeked, but now unmistakably like a public toilet.

The window would only open three inches, no matter how much I pounded on it. At least that was good for security, unless of course the intruder were serious, in which case he'd simply break the window.

CHAPTER FOURTEEN

Someone was rattling the padlock next door. I stuck my head out in time to see my next-door neighbor Lisa, securing her door. She looked about fourteen years old, but a well-worn fourteen. Bleached-blonde hair with a half-inch of brown roots formed a spiky halo around her childishly round face. Her fully adult body would be what paid her way. A see-through pink nylon wind breaker showed lush breasts, barely contained by a magenta elastic bra top. Her pink leatherette skirt hardly covered her crotch. I hurried out to the hall to intercept her.

"Hi, I just moved in here. Al told me I wasn't the only girl on her own here." Mistake. Her mouth twitched with hatred at the mention of Al.

"I'm Maggie. What's your name?"

"Lisa."

"I heard there used to be another single girl on this floor, in that room," I said, avoiding Al's name this time, and pointed at Kelly's door.

"She's gone."

"Did you know her?"

"We used to talk sometimes." Lisa wouldn't look at me. She kept her eyes on the toes of her glitter pink hightops. A hole was cut out of one to make room for a bulky bandage.

"Were you friends?"

"You don't have friends in a place like this. Nobody stays very long if they can help it. Ones who do stay, they ain't the kind you'd want to let in your room. They'd rip off your TV."

"But Kelly told you things."

"Why're you asking all these questions? You're police—are you vice?"

"No, I'm not a cop."

"Then why're you looking for Kelly?"

"I'm a private investigator."

"Yeah, right, and I'm Drew Fucking Barrymore."

"Here's my license." I pulled it out of my wallet and showed her. She held it close to her face to study. Either her vision or her reading ability was poor. I continued, "I've been hired to find out what happened to Kelly. I'm worried about her, and I want to help get her to a safe place."

"Yeah, well, I gotta go out and make some money." She limped toward the stairway, favoring the bandaged foot.

"I'll make you a business proposition. I'd like to buy your time."

"I don't do women." She jutted out her chin and took an aggressive stance.

"That's okay, all I want is to talk to you about Kelly. I'll pay you for that."

"I saw how you were looking at me."

"You guessed right—I'm a lesbian, but I like grown-ups. I don't have sex with girls your age. Where can we talk? If we stay here at the house, you can put your feet up."

"We can go to my room. I got a hot plate."

"I've got coffee and a filter cone. I'll make us some."

"And you're paying?"

"Twenty bucks for ten minutes."

Making coffee is a homey routine, even in a place like this, and we both let down our guard a notch or two as we located cups and something to use as a pot holder, fetched water from the hall bathroom and heated it, and finally poured it over the grounds. I told her it reminded me of the primitive plumbing we endured on the family farm growing up. As we burnt our mouths on too-hot brew, Lisa started telling me about her life.

She had been on her own for two years. When she turned twelve, her mother's boyfriend started coming to her bedroom while her mother was at work. Her mother wouldn't believe it was happening. The boyfriend brought some friends with him one night, and Lisa ran away the next day. Since then she'd lived off prostitution and, most likely, an occasional theft from a trick.

Lisa told me that Kelly was the only one in the house who ever talked to her. The women spat at her and cursed her in a variety of languages. Some of the men grabbed at her in the hall, and the rest ignored her. Al had demanded sex from her to let her move in, and whenever he wanted after that. Otherwise, he said, he'd turn her in to the juvenile authorities. He was the worst, because he looked like her mother's boyfriend.

"Tell me what Kelly was like—anything at all you remember."

"Like what?"

"Try shutting your eyes and getting a picture of her in your mind." She fluttered her lids half-closed, then sneaked a glance at me to make sure I wasn't trying to pull something. Finally she closed her eyes for real.

"Okay," I said, remembering how Tate had described inducing trance in her clients, "tell me what you see, and if you can remember any particular time you were together, try to bring back to mind what she said."

"She's . . . I think she's dead. When I think of her it's like 'she was,' not 'she is.'"

"Let's hope you're wrong, but I think we need to find her as soon as possible. If I were blind, how would you describe Kelly so I could recognize her?" There was a long silence, and I had given up on getting a response, when Lisa started crying.

"She was so sad—not just her expression. You could feel it. Disappointed. Not like missing a show you wanted to see, or somebody says they'll give you money or dope and they fuck you over. I could never tell how she was going to act when I saw her. Like one time when some dick-head almost killed me, she took care of me for three days. But afterwards she acted like it never happened, and like we weren't, you know, really friends." Another long silence.

"That's a lot of details nobody else could give me. You're good at this. Anything else?"

"I don't know how to say it . . . She didn't give off any heat."

"Heat?"

"She wasn't into sex at all. Some of the women been hookin' a long time, you get the same feeling, it's just business with them. But Kelly never turned tricks. She was all, 'no way would I do *that* with a man.' And she never talked about boyfriends—*or* girl-friends." She opened her eyes and glanced at me.

"This is exactly what I need, Lisa." I gave her an encouraging smile. "Tell me what Kelly looks like."

"Um . . . About my size. I think she's maybe 24, 25, 'cause of the music she likes—old stuff. She's got the best hair, wavy with a lot of body, you know, the way girls spend a ton of money to get with a perm? But she always yanks it back tight. I'd go, 'why don't you take off the rubber band, you'd look so hot,' but she was all, 'It doesn't make any difference.' And she has excellent skin. I bet she never had zits when she was my age."

"She isn't interested in looking good?"

"No, and it pissed me off! I'd go, 'Kelly, you could model, get out of those shitty jobs, if you'd work on yourself.'"

"Do you think she didn't want people to notice her?"

"No. I think it's . . . she's got so much on her mind, she

forgets to care how she looks."

"What do you think she mainly had on her mind?"

"Money, for sure. Who doesn't? And she was in therapy, she talked about that."

"Did she talk about her therapist?"

"Yeah, she told me this old dyke—I mean, lesbian—therapist was making her go down on her *and* making Kelly pay for it! She tells me this and I go, 'you liar!' I didn't believe her at first, but the things she told me . . . after awhile, I did believe her." Lisa eyed me surreptitiously to see how I was taking this, then continued. "That was sick shit, but I guess it's not any stranger than doin' guys who never wash. I can't believe how rank some of them are. You've got to do drugs to be able to stand the johns, so you can make enough off the johns to pay for your high. Kelly said the shrink told her she had to do it to get well. I couldn't see what she got out of it, though. She was real unhappy."

"Can you think of anyone she was afraid of? Anybody who might want to hurt her?"

"No, but from what she said, there was some people who should've been afraid of her! People she'd as soon kill as look at. She never said their names. One was a man, an old guy. I thought it might be her dad or her stepdad, like me. There was some woman, too. She only talked about 'her' once, when she thought I was too coked out to know what she was talkin' about. But it's funny, I can remember things like that later, even when I was wasted."

"You said you thought maybe it was her dad that she hated so much—did she ever talk about her family, or where she grew up?"

"Nothing. It was like she came from nowhere."

"How about visitors? Did anybody come see her here?"

"I heard voices in her room a couple of times. The walls in this place are about a half-inch thick."

"Male or female?"

"I'm not sure. Wait—She did have a guy here one time, really lame-looking."

"Can you describe him?"

"He had a hat pulled down on his face, like he was some TV star trying to hide out, like anybody in this place would care! Also, his mustache had to be fake. He was about your age, I guess, built-up, like he goes to the gym every day, but he was all hunched down to make himself small. I figured he was a fag. For sure he wasn't a boyfriend. There was no chemistry there."

"Did you meet him?"

"No, I just saw her let him into her room. I was takin' a guy up to my room, so I was kinda busy at the time."

"You've been a big help, Lisa." I put a twenty-dollar bill in her hand.

She inspected the bill, stuck it in the shoe that hadn't been cut open, then squinted at me. "Who'd this come from? You ain't layin' out your own money for this."

"That's confidential. It's my job to find Kelly, but if it turns out she dropped out of sight because she's in danger, well, I'd be inclined to forget where she went. Did you ever see her journal?"

"She told me about it, but she never let me near it. She was real touchy about it."

"Was there anyone else here that Kelly talked to?"

"I don't know. If there was, she didn't tell me. Uh . . . What would I have to do for you to give me fifty dollars?"

I handed her a pocket-sized notebook and one of my cards. "Here. Any time you think of something about Kelly, write it down. Then find me or call me the first chance you get. I'll give you a hundred dollars if we find her, and fifty even if we don't."

"Okay. I better go out now." She winced as she put her full weight on the injured foot. "These ugly shoes ain't too good for business."

"You look great! They won't even see the shoes."

I drove back to my cottage. It was less than twenty blocks away, but it felt like another universe. While I showered, I kept remembering details from my talk with Lisa. My impression of Kelly was changing once more. She acted like a compassionate older sister to Lisa, but held her at a distance. Much of what Lisa had told me supported the story Kelly told in the journal. But the journal made no mention of the man or woman Lisa told me that Kelly hated so intensely. Could they be Kelly's parents? Then there was the Kelly who emerged from my conversation with the women from Nature's Harmony, a spy who welcomed Jerry Reardon's sexual advances. That was completely at odds with Lisa's description of her.

If Kelly seemed to be several women, Moira Ericson was a complete unknown. My first knee-jerk assumption that the accuser must be the victim was transforming to a doubt that a lesbian therapist who had been a classmate of my friend Tate could do such a thing.

"For crying out loud," Jack's voice intruded, "why don't you just do the job for a change? It doesn't matter who's the good guy, and it's none of your business anyway. I never let that stuff bother me." I've got a question for you, Jack: Why'd you have to drink yourself to death? I could've used a few more years as your junior associate.

It might be unprofessional, it might get me fired, but I needed to meet Moira, and either come to peace with this case or quit.

Before I could give it any pragmatic consideration, I looked up her office number in the directory and dialed. Memories of trying to call my own therapist made me expect a machine or a service. Moira picked up herself, and I was temporarily at a loss for what to say. Then training and habit clicked in. I explained who I was and what her family had hired me to do. To my amazement she agreed to meet me Thursday evening in her office.

Moira Ericson sounded just like my second-grade teacher, Mrs. Gillespie. Moira's voice had the same combination of affection and condescension that some people adopt for babies and puppies. What would have fit my preconceptions: seductiveness, verbal bondage and domination?

When the phone rang, my hand was still resting on it. I screeched and dropped it. The cool-headed Ms. Garrett was a bit skittish tonight. It was Diana, apologizing for being late. She'd be out front in fifteen minutes. I didn't admit that I'd lost track of time and wasn't ready. If we became an item, I'd confess some day. I hung up and ran to the bedroom. What to wear? After trying and discarding a heap of clothes, I put on a short black lycra skirt and an ivory lace wrapped-front blouse with a distinguished track record. It dipped when I moved, showing a delicate camisole that had been an excellent wardrobe investment. I'd have to remember to bend over frequently.

I was having second thoughts about how Diana would handle the message this outfit would be conveying (okay, hollering) when she rang the doorbell.

CHAPTER FIFTEEN

This was not how our second date was supposed to end. Diana was driving me home, her eyes and attention on the road. She was stiff with tension, and I'd become tense too, without knowing what was going on.

The beginning of the evening was promising. My friend Erroll had used everything left in his bank account for the grand opening of Hedy's, his dream restaurant. The tables were far enough apart to give the illusion of privacy, and the lighting was intimate. A jazz quartet played Cole Porter ballads with humor and affection. I think the food must have been extraordinary, although I can't remember what I ate.

Diana and I filled in details of our lives and life stories. It felt right. I didn't have to censor what I said. Diana didn't look down on me for being a P.I., and she shared my fascination with what makes people act like heroes or monsters. Erroll brought us gardenias and glasses of champagne, and we toasted each other. We laughed easily and often. Couples at other tables gave us envious looks.

But as the evening wore on Diana drew more and more into her own thoughts, giving absent replies when I tried to get the conversation going again. By the time we paid the check she was politely cordial. I made nervous small talk and racked my brain: What had I said, what had I done?

Now we were in front of my house. Diana pulled the car up to the curb and sat looking ahead, both hands on the wheel. She wasn't even going to turn the engine off. Say something!

"Would you like to come in?" Look in her eyes, don't be such a coward!

"Thanks, but I'd better go home. I have to be at work at six tomorrow. Besides, I think we should go slow—that is, if we're going anywhere." She was giving me that lopsided smile that had stayed with me after our first meeting months ago.

"Okay . . . Maybe we could do this again soon?"

"Sure."

"Well, I had a great time . . . ." I leaned slightly toward her, as she leaned toward me. Our lips brushed, and then brushed again. If either of us had moved away at that moment, the evening might have ended there. It could almost have been a social kiss, a friendly goodbye.

We looked at each other. Each could see the hesitation—to leave, to stay, to take chances—mirrored in the other's eyes. Our lips met again, tentatively. This kiss was braver.

"Are you sure you don't want to come in?" I said, brushing a curl out of her eyes.

"There's something safe about sitting here in the car, still at the beginning part, where I can tell myself 'hey, it's only a kiss.' I can relax and just be here with you." She turned off the ignition, eased out of her jacket, and threw it into the back seat. "Could we just make out a little?"

Her lower lip trembled slightly as she spoke. In the time-honored tradition of besotted lovers, I decided that the lower lip was my favorite. I drew it into my mouth.

"Does the beginning include anything besides kissing? I was just wondering," I asked, and kissed the outer edge of her cheek below her eye. Already my hands of their own volition were moving over her wide shoulders, getting acquainted with the muscles on her arms, delighting in her surprisingly delicate collarbone. I wanted to take in every part of her, but not at the risk of ending this moment.

"Remember making out in junior high school? We had all the thrills without the fear of catching diseases or causing any damage." She fastened her lips on my neck. I'd have a hickey the next day. I didn't care.

"You were much more precocious than me," I panted. "I didn't even make out until high school, and it was only with boys. I didn't graduate to women until college."

"Let me show you some things you missed." She reached under my waistband and slid her hand beneath my blouse. Her fingers lightly traced the skin under my camisole straps, which felt especially sensitized. Then, thrillingly, she explored the X-rated, forbidden unknown of Junior High. My right nipple hardened in anticipation when her fingers were inches away.

Diana was right, this concentration on certain areas and certain actions brought an intense eroticism that I had forgotten. I was profoundly aroused by touches I would hardly notice if we were naked in bed.

There was a world of sensuality in the opening of my blouse. Diana unfastened the knot at my waist, and the silky lace fell away.

"You wore this blouse to drive me crazy didn't you?" she whispered huskily into my ear. "I couldn't keep my eyes off it all evening. You don't play fair, Maggie Garrett."

The perfume of crushed gardenias filled the car, as we bruised the delicate petals of the flowers Erroll had given us. Diana bent to kiss my collarbone. She lifted up the camisole to expose my breasts, caressing me with the satin. A delicious shiver passed through me. We both made soft "ahh" sounds as she cupped my breasts, easily covering them with her large hands, and catching the nipples between her fingers.

She lowered her mouth first to my right breast, then the left, kissing, tasting, nipping lightly. I caught my breath, and let it out on a ragged moan. Exquisite pleasure in the sensation of her mouth turned into craving for more.

"You make me feel things again, and that terrifies me." She spoke so quietly I could hardly hear her. What could make this fierce, accomplished woman so afraid?

I rose to kneel sideways on the seat, and she moved to face me in the same position. Then I took her in my arms and laid her back on the seat.

Slowly I undid the buttons on her starched shirt, often lingering on the supple skin underneath. I pushed aside the stiff fabric. Her breasts were enclosed in a sheer wisp of tan and ivory lace. I began to laugh, picturing her debating whether to wear this while I was considering the camisole. She covered my mouth with hers and the laugh turned into a sigh of desire.

The light from a passing car revealed brown areolas through the pattern of the lace. The bra was cut low, and I only had to pull down a bit of the fragile fabric to partially expose one of her nipples. As I bent to take it between my teeth, she arched her back, bringing her breast higher, and the dark nipple rose to meet my mouth.

Diana called out my name. Her hands had been moving over my body with practiced skill. Now her touch took on a frenzied quality. Her bra had a single front hook, for which I gave thanks as I unfastened it.

Her generous white breasts spilled out, and I balanced their weight like ripened fruit in my palms. My tongue traced the path of a blue vein visible more in my imagination than in the dim street light, then rimmed the lovely brown circle on her other breast. She writhed in response and I fastened my lips to her nipple and followed the movement of her body.

My right hand slid down her stomach past the waistband of

her slacks. Another praise to the goddess of love that it was loose enough for me to get my hand inside. How soft her skin was!

I asked her in a whisper if this was still what she wanted. Wordlessly she took my left hand and kissed my palm, sucked hard on my fingertips. I caressed her lower belly as my hand inched toward those other lips. She shifted to help me reach farther down. We were moving beyond the safe beginning, at last. This woman belonged in my life and in my bed. It had taken half of a year to get this far, and I was set on convincing her to make that leap tonight.

When her beeper sounded, we both jumped as if an electrical shock rather than a rude noise had intruded.

"Damn." It was a complete statement. Diana was leaning into her bra cups and covering up those glorious breasts. She kept her eyes averted. As I had hoped, she'd be coming into my house, but it was only to use the telephone.

I tried lightness: "Can we start all over again—soon? I think it may take a lot of this to make up for my deprived adolescence."

"Glad to help out," she said into my neck, and we went into the house.

Eavesdropping on her end of the phone conversation, I gathered that there had been a domestic dispute, which ended in the husband's taking a fatal plunge down a flight of stairs. I recognized the surviving spouse's name: she was a local TV newscaster. Kid glove material, an assignment for a classy female homicide detective like Diana. I watched her straighten her clothing and apply lipstick in the mirror next to my front door, trying to think of the right words to say. She arranged her features into an impassive cop facade and turned when she saw me watching her.

"Well, that's why I like to keep it all at the beginning. It's hard to maintain a relationship when this kind of thing is a normal occurrence." By the time she spoke the last words she seemed so far away that she might as well be gone.

I grabbed her departing shoulders and spun her around to face me. "Diana, don't do this." I tried to kiss her but she ducked away. "Please don't shut me out."

"I can't go through this again, I don't have anything left. You can't know, Maggie." There were tears at the corners of her eyes.

"I know we were magic tonight. We laugh at the same things, we respect each other. I know that if anyone is in a position to understand each other's crazy jobs, it's the two of us!"

"I have to go. I'll call you," she answered, giving me a bleak glance before turning away. I watched the receding tail lights of her car. The gray van that had been circling the block earlier was parked a few doors up from my house.

My answering machine had an agitated message from Chad, my friend at the Glass agency. I dialed the number he had given, and Chad picked up immediately. He told me that he and Paolo were off the Ericson case. Roy Glass had told them, with considerable spleen, about the Ericsons' decision to limit their business to my agency.

"Paolo and I've been worried about you, Maggie. Somebody else is working a surveillance van in the vicinity of your girl's house."

"I have noticed that someone is fascinated by my every move. Do you know who it is?"

"Paolo thought he recognized Dougie Mays. Dougie's with Parker Security."

"I always thought the Ericsons were hedging their bets by using both you guys and me. Maybe they fired you because they figured out we're friends."

"But why do all this counter-espionage stuff? We weren't supposed to be spying on you. Anyway, why wouldn't they trust you?"

"Chad, I'm not sure *I'd* trust me to act in the Ericsons' interests. Thanks for telling me, I owe you one. Tomorrow I'm going to call Robert Summers and ask him what the hell he's doing."

"Don't call him yet. Let me do a little checking first. That way, you can tell Summers what you know, instead of asking him. That'd be a much better position to deal from."

"You're a genius. OK, I'll hold off 'til I hear from you. Thanks again, Chad."

It was only eleven o'clock. Liam might be out for hours. Or if he and Sam were having a showdown, he might not be back at all. It was too late to call Jessie, who was an early riser. The espresso I'd drunk after dinner was kicking in, and I was left wide awake, trying to figure out how to make Diana see reason. It was not a rewarding exercise.

CHAPTER SIXTEEN

I sniffed the air for Spinelli's Viennese blend. Nothing but faint doggy odor and the potpourri my youngest sister sends me every Christmas. It was time to get up, with or without a coffee bribe.

A contented chorus of purrs, snores and snorts came from the assembly sleeping on and around the couch. Liam's long form was curved around Fearless, who was curled into a ball. They wore similar beatific expressions. Pod was draped over the back of the couch, his paw resting on Liam's shoulder. On the floor next to the couch, Pugsley reposed on a bed made of Liam's neatly folded clothes.

Liam stirred, stretched and sat up when he saw me.

"Hi sweets, how was your date?"

"She had to go to a crime scene."

"Wait! Isn't that what happened the last time?"

"Yeah, but we were, um, farther along than last time."

"I see." He grinned and waggled his eyebrows. "As a matter of fact, I see a love bite the size of Montana on your neck, so things *have* advanced." He patted the cushion next to him. "Sit down, tell all. What's the verdict?"

"She's commitment-shy. I think she must be getting over a bad relationship. She practically ran out the door." We looked at each other. "I'm not ready to give up yet."

"That's a good sign. Normally if anything at all goes wrong, you decide the two of you were never meant to be. When do I get to meet her?"

"Not anytime soon. Maybe never. You'd get all gooey about what a cute couple we are, and she'd really be scared off. So, Liam, how come there's no coffee?"

"We're out. Want some mint tea?"

I won't go into what I said or what I almost said. Our friendship survived, and I got out of the house much faster than usual.

I arrived at my office building so early that I had to pick my way among the sleeping forms of the homeless men and women who camp in the lobby and plaza outside, trying not to spill my Spinelli's grande latte. It was just as well that I had a head start on the day. My first official report to Summers was due, ridiculous as that was in fact, since I talked to both of the Ericsons practically every hour on the hour.

Ricardo wouldn't be in, so there'd be no distractions, no requests for an assessment of whether his skin was clearing up, no arguments over whose day it was to decide what the office boombox would play.

He had, bless him, picked up my order from the photo shop down the street. The Nature's Harmony Foods group photo was cropped to show only Kelly, and enlarged. The reproduction was even grainier than I'd expected, but it was all we had. I stuck a dozen copies in my bag, and used one to make up a photocopied flyer offering a reward for information about her.

I finally ran out of these stalling maneuvers, and the Ericsons' report still wasn't written. After ten minutes of staring at the computer screen, on which I had so far entered only the day's date and my clients' names, I picked up Kelly's journal.

August 7. I was talking about my mother today, and Moira stopped me and asked if I ever told anybody else about the work we do together. She said it was important to keep it a secret until her book comes out. I told her I didn't have anybody to talk to. I'm afraid she can tell I'm lying. I tell people about my therapy because it's the only important thing in my life.

August 9. Today she asked me to take off all my clothes. I did it, but I kept my eyes shut the whole time. She was excited. I could hear her breathing hard. I didn't want to undress like that, but I kept thinking about what happened when I said I didn't want to kiss her. It felt like I was going to die waiting for her to forgive me.

August 16. After I took my clothes off today she had me stand in front of the mirror and touch myself. She said I needed to experience my sexuality. I said I couldn't do that. She turned her back on me and wouldn't talk to me anymore.

August 19. I don't know what to think about what happened today. Moira put me in front of the mirror again. She said I was afraid to make the next step to get well, and I needed help to get in touch with my body. She came over behind me and took my hand and put it on my bush.

August 18. Patrick is the only caller I talk to very much. He said what Moira is doing is wrong, that she doesn't care about helping me. I got mad and left. But when I'm alone later I think maybe something isn't right. Then I feel bad, because Moira says I'm her favorite client, and she thinks about me when she's with the other ones, who don't really want to get well.

August 26. I didn't sleep for two days, thinking about what she said, that I have to give my trust to her completely to get well. Yesterday I told her I was ready. She showed me what to do. Afterwards she asked me if I'd liked it. I said yes. She said she was so proud of my progress. Since then I've felt worse. I must be crazier than she thinks.

*Sept. 1. I told her I didn't have enough money to see her three times
a week anymore. I asked if I could pay her over time, but she had
another idea. Would I like to work for her at her house? I asked what
kind of work, and she said cleaning and cooking, one day for every
time I had a session. I said I also had to work at my jobs to be able
to eat and pay rent. She sent me home to think about my priorities.*

Could a lesbian therapist do this to a client? A voice in my
head screamed NO. However, reason intruded, there's no deny-
ing that gay men and women sometimes turned out as vile as the
worst of the general population. We had produced a few serial
killers. Moira might be one of those deeply disturbed souls who
manage to conceal their true personality for years. Maybe she
went over the edge when she had this guileless woman in her
power.

But Kelly was far from guileless, according to nearly everyone I talked to about her. Even Kelly's friend Lisa saw her as
shaping her own life. Then why had she portrayed herself as a
victim in the journal, and why had she disappeared? Questions
kept whirring around in my mind like small, irritable animals.

Half an hour left to write the report to Summers. I tran-
scribed my notes, omitting my meetings with Howard and Sylvia
Ericson, printed two copies, and stuck one of them in a manila
envelope for Robert Summers. The other I put on Ricardo's
desk so he could read it before he filed it according to his own
esoteric system. I called for a Lickety Split bike messenger to
pick up Summers' envelope from the lobby guard, and left for
another morning at Nature's Harmony Foods.

CHAPTER SEVENTEEN

GT, the Nature's Harmony produce manager, had the entrance of the store blockaded with what looked like cardboard boxes swathed in heavy plastic garbage bags. I said hello on my way in. He growled a response but didn't look up as he hauled several of the bulky items to the pickup double-parked out front. Patty left her cash register to close the door, which was letting in a chilly breeze.

"What's with GT?" I asked.

"Jerry told him he had to make a dump run before the store opened today. GT didn't do it, and Jerry threw a fit. GT says, 'It's not part of my job.' So Jerry goes, 'If you want to keep working, you better think of anything I tell you to do as part of your job.' So GT's doing it, but I'd keep away from him for the rest of the day if I were you."

"Why not let Sunset Scavengers haul it off with the rest of the garbage?"

"They'd charge extra. I think Jerry's idea of a dump run is dropping your trash in somebody else's dumpster. Jerry's real cheap."

Or real sneaky. If Jerry was too cheap to leave the boxes for the scavenger company, why use expensive heavy plastic bags to wrap them? I waited until GT drove off and walked to the back of the store. Jerry's door was shut, and except for a lone checker at the front, everyone had gone off for coffee. I snooped around the room off the produce area, poking in and under garbage cans, in corners. In the third can, I hit pay dirt: a paper bag containing dozens of the flexible metal strips that growers use to hold certain varieties of lettuces together, imprinted with the trademark of a Central Valley grower that was frequently attacked by farmworkers' groups for using risky pesticides.

"What are you doing?" Someone asked from the doorway.

I turned to face my accuser. It was Leslie, who had become so agitated at lunch the day before.

"I'm looking for what Kelly was so interested in. And I think I may have found it." I held up one of the twisties. "Do you know about this?"

Leslie examined it and made a face. "I didn't know about it, but for all I know, everything in this place is from Food-4-Less. What do these things have to do with Kelly?"

"If word got out that Jerry is passing off non-organic produce as the real thing, how much trouble would he be in?"

"I don't know if he'd go to jail, but it would wipe out the business. There's a certain amount of trust involved in buying organic food. An orange pretty much looks like an orange, but the ones here can cost five times as much because they don't have chemicals in them. If people don't believe that our oranges are organic, there's plenty of other places they can go."

"Could this be what Kelly was holding over Jerry? Or was it his sexual harassment?"

The bell hooked up to the door rang. Leslie peeked around the corner to see who had entered the store. "It's Daryl and Patty," she said. "I'm due for a break in ten minutes, after the others get back. I'll meet you at the coffee shop on the corner."

When we were face to face at a formica table, weak coffee poured and scones in hand, Leslie took a deep drink from her cup and told her story.

"I knew Kelly outside the store. I met her in a group we both went to."

"A 12-step group?"

"Yes. I don't talk about it at work. They aren't Program people."

"Have you seen her lately?"

"No, not since the last day she was at work. Is she . . . Has something happened to her?"

"I don't know. Everything I hear about her contradicts what the person before told me. I am worried about her. Tell me anything you can that might help me find her."

"I could see that something was up between her and Jerry. First he acted like he'd just won the lottery when word got around that Kelly was having sex with him. But then later he'd act jumpy whenever she was around. Cecelia was right, Jerry looked relieved when she didn't show up for work."

"Would Jerry have been willing to pay Kelly to keep her quiet about the produce?"

"I don't know, but for sure he can't afford to screw up again. He used to have his own business, but he wasn't any good at it, and he went bankrupt. So now he works as a manager for the Nature's Harmony stores. Last week I was in his office and saw a couple of letters they sent him. This is his last chance."

"Did Kelly ever mention her therapy to you?"

"No, all I heard was that she was having sex with her therapist, and that was so strange, because—" Leslie paused and impatiently pushed a lock of hair out of her eyes. "Most of what I know about Kelly, she said in the ISA group, and that's supposed to be confidential."

I made noncommittal, encouraging sounds, but my brain reeled, taking in what she had just said. ISA stands for Incest Survivors Anonymous. Kelly's diary didn't mention incest at all, but her abuser could be a potential suspect in her disappearance.

"Leslie, I've been around a lot of 12-step people," I said, treading carefully around this hyper-sensitive topic. "As I understand them, the 12-step principles are to protect people who are honest enough to admit that they have a problem. I think you have to decide what you believe would be best for Kelly."

"In ISA she called herself Judy. She never shared very much." Leslie paused, bit her lip, and continued. "But I do remember one thing she said. She shared that she couldn't be sexual with anybody since the time she was incested. She couldn't even stand to be touched. Then she came to work at the store, and told everybody her name was Kelly. She acted totally different here than in the ISA meetings. After a couple of weeks, every time you turned around, Jerry would be grabbing her breasts, or rubbing his thing against her. And she *let* him." She shuddered. "That's why the others hate her. Kelly let him do it to her."

"I saw a picture of the two of them. Jerry was all over her. She looked terribly unhappy."

"Jerry doesn't care if you like it. If he can get a woman to hold still, he's satisfied."

"So, was it true, what Patty and Cecelia said about Kelly having sex with Jerry?"

"Who knows? There's always gossip like that around here. Like they're saying you must be doing it with him . . . are you?"

"Of course not! Why would they say that?"

"Because Jerry told GT you like to give him head, the same way he said Kelly did, and GT passed it on. Kelly never denied it."

"So Jerry comes off as the big stud. Well, regardless of what Kelly—or Judy—was or wasn't doing with Jerry, she did say that she was having sex with her therapist. Did she talk to you about that?"

"No, GT told everybody in the store after she told him about it."

"What did you think was going on? Did you ever ask her?"

"Kelly never talked to me after she started working here. At first I figured she was avoiding me, then I realized that I've lost about forty pounds in the last five months, and I always used to wear dark glasses in the meetings. She didn't recognize me! I thought maybe she'd changed her name as part of working through her incest. A lot of incest survivors change their names. I didn't say anything to her, and after she started acting so weird . . . I don't know how to explain it. I was embarrassed that I knew about her, like *I'd* done something wrong!"

"Why would she confide in GT about the therapist? He's the last person I'd confide in about my personal life."

"Yeah, I know. That was part of what was so weird. The only reason I could think of was her own self-hatred, since GT loves ugly gossip."

Or if she wanted to make sure that the gossip was spread for her own purposes.

"Leslie, I need a favor."

"What?" She shot me an apprehensive glance.

"Are you in contact with any of the women from the ISA group where you met Judy?"

"I've got a couple of their phone numbers . . . ."

"Could you call and see if they know anything about her? Her last name, where she was from, anyone else who might know her?"

"No, that's impossible! Program principles don't allow that kind of thing. A year or so ago they subpoenaed a whole AA meeting after a guy shared that he'd killed somebody. Ever since then, people have been super-cautious about giving out information, because somebody might sue somebody else. Program people don't break confidentiality."

"Program people don't generally disappear after saying that their therapist is abusing them, either. Please?"

"I guess I could say I need to contact her, and it's urgent." She made rings on the table with her coffee cup. "Okay," she said, "give me your number and I'll call you from home."

I gave her my home and office numbers. Back at the store, I spent an uneventful morning putting new stickers with higher prices and later pull dates onto gourmet foods. At the end of my shift I stuck an apple and a small chunk of cheese in my pocket and paid for a rosemary roll and bottle of water on my way out the door. I took my picnic to a small neighborhood park and found a dry patch on the grass.

On a bench fifty feet away sat two muscular men dressed as tourists, their shorts revealing too much scary-white leg flesh (the rest of their get-ups included camera, binoculars, and sweatshirts with pictures of the Golden Gate Bridge). They were watching me and trying to look like they weren't. The quality of Parker Security operatives was commensurate with their notoriously low pay. I waved at them as I stashed my garbage in a can and dusted crumbs off my clothes. They scowled at me and started gathering up their props.

The sun had come out, and it was turning into one of those gorgeous hot days we get in October. A day when everyone who can get away with it calls in sick and heads for the beach. Not me. There was less than an hour before Job Number Two at the Symphony, and Patrick might be working today. I shut out thoughts of sand and water and set off in search of a phone booth, my office away from the office.

First I called Chad about the guys shadowing me. They were beginning to work my nerves. He told me that, according to the gossip mill at Glass, Howard Ericson had expressed a lack of confidence in that agency. All Chad had been able to glean from his contact at Parker was that the agency had a new case, top-secret, involving four contract agents. I thanked him and hung up.

Sounded like the Ericsons to me. It was highly unlikely that

Robert Summers, Esq., was involved. The Ericsons must be side-stepping their attorney again, perhaps this time in tandem rather than behind each other's backs. I dialed their hotel suite.

Sylvia Ericson answered. She made me repeat my details of being shadowed three times, complaining that the street noise outside my phone booth made it impossible to understand me. Her speech had the elaborate caution of the very drunk. I watched as a fastidiously dressed white man with an Operation Rescue bumper sticker on his Pontiac double-parked and trundled in my direction, fishing in his pockets. The occupant of the other phone booth, a cute African-American man with a rhinestone rainbow on his leather cap, was watching him, too. Our eyes met, and we exchanged evil grins.

"I'll speak with Howard about it this evening, Maggie. I'm sure it will all turn out to be a mistake."

"Thank you Sylvia, I'll talk to you soon."

"Wait, I'm not finished. I was going to call you anyway. Can you meet me tonight, say six o'clock? I have to talk with you, but privately, not on the phone like this."

"All right, how about if I come to your hotel?" She didn't sound as if she could make her way out of her boudoir.

"No! This is related to our personal arrangement. Privacy is of the utmosh—the utmost importance." The more she slurred, the more icy her dignity became. She gave me the address of a cocktail lounge less than a block from her hotel.

"Have to hang up now. . . need to rest." She hung up.

The Operation Rescue man was pacing ostentatiously outside the phone booths, making it clear that he was seriously inconvenienced. The caller in the other booth was in the middle of intense negotiations. From his facial expressions and hand gestures, I guessed that he was pleading for another chance with somebody.

One last call, just to tweak the Operation Rescue man, because of that streak of cussedness: I left a long message for Ricardo about checking on Kelly's alias as Judy. Not much to go on, but we'd done miracles with less.

CHAPTER EIGHTEEN

Being a satisfactory employee for the Western Symphony was low on my list of priorities for the day. My main objective was to talk with Patrick, the man Kelly mentioned in her journal. I settled into a calling station with a cup of bad coffee, a computer printout of numbers to call, scripted pitches, brochures on special series packages and a phonetic spelling sheet of words like *leitmotiv*.

First I called my office. The machine fed back to me confirmation of dinner Friday night with Jessie and Tate and their neighbor. The date and time had been rescheduled several times, which reinforced my ambivalence about the evening. Relax, I told myself, don't think too much about it. Life-changing events could occur between now and Friday night: an earthquake, a broken leg, winning millions at Lotto. Who knew, by then I might be going for another drive with Diana.

All this went through my mind while I played an incoherent rant from a prospective female client, asking whether I trailed unfaithful sons of bitches, but forgetting to leave her phone number.

Liam wasn't answering at my house, and that machine tape contained only a brusque request from Diana to give her some time, "I don't know if I'm ready for someone like you—I'm sorry," ending with a request not to call her.

She was dismissing me. A scalding wave of anger and hurt washed over me. I wanted to go confront her and make her say it to my face, or at least lock myself in the Women's Room and kick the stalls a few times. Instead I went to work.

My calling list contained hundreds of phone numbers, which according to Roxane belonged to people with a history of attending the Symphony. Maybe their ancestors had. Mostly I got that maddening computer-voice "No Longer in Service" message and answering machines. I did have one long, chatty conversation with an elderly woman who bought a matinee series for herself and a neighbor, and was rewarded by getting a three-dollar cash bonus. This was thrilling out of all proportion to the paltry amount, like finding money on the street. My name was scrawled on the blackboard of honor, though without exclamation marks. That was for big sales. If the P.I. business goes under, I thought, there's an exciting future for me in telemarketing.

Then I reached a woman, from her tone a high-level executive, at work. She was furious that she had been interrupted by a mere phone solicitor and demanded to know where I got her number. Without pausing to hear my answer, she insisted on speaking with my supervisor. I repeated my explanation more loudly. She called me a pushy bitch. I hung up on her. Even if she called back, and even if the Symphony cared enough to investigate, it would take time to expose me as the culprit.

Surely it was time for Patrick to take a smoking break. I picked up the pack of Carltons I had bought for the occasion and went outside. It was easy to identify the man leaning against a wall in the shade of a scraggly urban tree as Patrick. My nameless informant had described his Kaposi's sarcoma lesions. He wore clothes that were several sizes too large, pants cinched with a belt and hanging loose on his slight body. He was talking intently with another man. As I drew closer, I could make out phrases about protocols and clinical trials. Patrick was giving a comprehensive background on a new experimental treatment for HIV.

I hovered near the two, hesitant to start a conversation with one of the other members of the nicotine community and miss my chance with Patrick if the other man went in first. Both men put out their cigarettes and walked back in together. A real P.I. would have stepped in and interrupted the conversation. Jack Windsor had said this kind of wimping out was my second-worst weakness. The worst, of course, was my reluctance to pack steel.

Oh well, there was always the next break. I moved to a calling station where I could keep an eye on the exit, and dialed again. More machines, and disconnected numbers, interspersed with rude refusals to talk. Sometimes I hear people brag about the witty putdowns they use on telemarketers. From now on, nobody better boast about blowing a whistle into the phone while I was around. Two dismal, no-bonus hours went by. Everyone seemed to be having a excruciatingly bad day—even the veterans whose names I had seen on the blackboard with stars and exclamation marks. Roxane came by with a tray of cookies and words of encouragement for everybody. Finally I saw Patrick going out the door, a pack of Marlboro Lights in hand.

I followed on his heels and asked him for a light before he could start a conversation with anyone else. He told me that he'd noticed me watching him earlier and assumed I was staring at his K.S. lesions. We traded best and worst answering machine messages of the day, and I told him about the vengeful woman executive.

"You did her a favor. Now she can put up with whatever her boss, or husband, or pool boy dishes out, and all because she tore into you, and then probably reached poor old Roxane and tore her up, too. Not to worry. You don't seem like the type to be here for long, anyway."

"You're right. I'm trying to find someone who used to work

here, Kelly Henry."

"Why're you looking for her?"

"She's been missing for almost three weeks."

"Okay, but, why are *you* looking for her? Are you a relative, a girlfriend, what?"

"I'm a private investigator." I showed him my license, since he was nobody's fool. "I'm also worried about her. Do you know her?"

He studied the license longer than anyone ever had.

"You could've bought this at Woolworth's for all I know, but I choose to believe you, Margaret Garrett. I couldn't say I knew her. She was like quicksilver. But yes, we used to talk during breaks like this."

"Did she tell you about her therapist?"

"Oh yes. It was about the second thing out of her mouth when we met. Some people do that with therapy, make it their major conversation topic. But with Kelly, there was something different. Like she'd always use the therapist's name when she talked about her. Everybody else just says 'my therapist' or 'my shrink.'"

"Did she ever talk to you about the content of her therapy?"

"You mean, did she say she was having sex with her therapist and cleaning the therapist's house to pay for the privilege? Yes she did."

"You don't mince words, do you?"

"I don't have the time to mince, anymore. She told me her story, but frankly, I didn't buy it. Mind you, her delivery was marvelous. I can't put my finger on what exactly it was, but I've spent my whole life sifting through bullshit, and this young thing was telling me less than the complete truth, as they say."

"But why would she do that? Assuming it wasn't true, why would she—"

"—bother with me? You gotta wonder. I don't have any

money, I'm obviously not a candidate for a boyfriend. Not that she had a sexual aura about her, anyway. She wasn't happy where she was living, but I live in a room in the Tenderloin, and I'm not looking for a roommate. So what's left?"

"You're entertaining. Maybe it's as simple as that. Why did *you* keep talking to *her?*"

"The mystery of it all! Coming to this place is the most exciting thing I do all day." Patrick flicked his ashes in the direction of an overflowing receptacle. "I thought if she kept going, she'd slip and I'd figure out her angle. Besides, I liked her, even though I suspected she had some powerful homophobia close to the surface." He lit another cigarette from the first. Noting my disapproval, he snorted. "Yeah, yeah, it's bad for me. But every time I quit, the stress of detoxing zaps my T-cell count. And the threat of lung cancer isn't as scary as it used to be."

"When was the last time you saw Kelly?"

"Hmmm . . . The weeks run together at this place, and I work random shifts depending on my health. I know Roxane comes across as an animated Barbie doll, but she's been good to me, lets me just show up on the days when I feel good." He puffed thoughtfully for a few seconds. "Last time I saw Kelly I'd just switched meds, so that's three weeks ago."

"Did you notice anything different about Kelly the last time you saw her?"

"She was a little more up than usual. I figured she'd managed to convince another poor sucker to go for that European Masters deal—you know, the premier series where the ticket includes having cocktails with the first violinist, while the composer gives you a foot rub? Kelly could charm those old folks into buying tickets for composers and artists they'd never heard of."

"Roxane said Kelly was good, too. Other people had given me the impression that she was shy, and so helpless that I wondered how she survived."

"Hmmm. You wouldn't want to be in Kelly's way when she's got a live one on the hook! Speaking of which. . . ." He turned to go.

I gave Patrick my card in case he thought of anything else, and a check for a hundred dollars for being a source. He gave me a glorious grin, and sang, "I do believe in private eyes, I do!" as he returned to the building.

I'd have to do some fancy footwork to get that expenditure reimbursed, but buying Patrick a couple of days off with the Ericsons' money felt so good that it would be worth the hassles.

My shift was supposed to last until six o'clock, but at five I packed it in. Roxane inspected my totals, gave me a weak smile and urged me to "try extra hard" the next time. This must be her mild version of putting me on notice. I didn't tell her that, since I had spoken with Patrick, I probably wouldn't be back.

On the way to my car I got that sensation of being watched again. I assumed my woman-warrior demeanor. Who knew? It could be Parker thugs or a free-lance mugger. No one in sight. I kept an eye on the rear-view mirror, and checked for familiar vehicles driving on parallel streets at each intersection. No one was following me.

I left flyers with Kelly's picture at the Women's Building and Metropolitan Community Church, the main sites for 12-step groups, and stapled them to nearby posts. Sometimes this most obvious of tactics worked. I had considered sitting in on meetings Kelly might have attended, but it would have been disrespectful of the people in them—and unlikely to get results because of the 12-step commitment to anonymity. Even Leslie's prospects for getting a last name for "Judy" looked slim.

It was one of those days when I missed my early career as a temp legal assistant. Put in your hours, go home, watch TV, do a little volunteer work. Sure, some of the attorneys were jerks, but

I didn't have to meet them at cocktail lounges, if they were un-ethical they were answerable to the Bar Association, and none of them ever had me followed, let alone tried to feel me up.

At a stop sign I watched two women in an ancient VW trade bites off an overstuffed burrito. The passenger ended up with guacamole on her nose. The driver, lovingly wiping it off, forgot to take her turn to cross the intersection. Then the car stalled. As horns behind them blared, the driver threw up her hands in surrender. She grabbed the burrito away from her companion and took a giant bite. On a typical day I would applaud. Today I hoped they got a ticket.

I knew why I was in such a foul mood. It was that message from Diana. I kept playing it over in my mind. Too bad I didn't have voicemail. I could have saved it and listened to it over and over for the nuances of her rejection: She secretly wished I'd come and ravage her? She was having a hormone day and prone to overstatement? She needed a few days' space? She never wanted to hear from me again? She never wanted to hear my name again?

Who says you need more than one dyke for dyke drama?

I did a double take passing a woman waiting at a bus stop and nearly clipped a cyclist. The woman looked uncannily like my friend Nikki Fong, who was holed up somewhere in Sonoma County. Nikki had retired from social life to nurse her grudge against Sarita for moving to Prague without her. Nikki believed that Sarita was her destiny, her soul mate, and measured every new woman by the impossible standard of the idealized Sarita. I had made one trip to see Nikki, but I knew I wouldn't go back: She wasn't much fun to be around these days. No, I would never be like that, even if—Another car almost sideswiped me and I came back to reality with a squeal of brakes.

CHAPTER NINETEEN

My house was blissfully quiet. Fearless and Pugsley haughtily ignored my arrival: I had been gone too much lately, and their trust had been betrayed. Pod sprang his full eighteen pounds onto my shoulder. He purred ecstatically and burrowed his nose into my hair, then sprang off toward his food dish with little cries of encouragement.

"Sycophantic suck-up," I muttered, opening a can of flaked salmon. "Is this the flavor I gave you this morning?" I don't know how Pod can remember or why he cares, but he rejects repeats.

After a quick shower, I made myself an omelette. Pugsley ended up with most of it. I told myself that meeting Moira was routine, no big deal. My appetite wouldn't oblige. Passages from Kelly's journal kept intruding on my peace of mind.

I put on the severe black suit I had bought for Grandma Faith's funeral. It made me look grown-up, hard-edged and almost butch, perfect for my meetings with Sylvia and Moira. I used the last of the coffee to wash down a couple of antacid tablets and stroked the head of each animal for luck.

"This is the glamour of the job, the pay-off," I told myself, while I tried to angle the Toyota into an impossibly small space four blocks from the cocktail lounge on Nob Hill where Sylvia would be waiting. "Driving off into the night to interview complex, potentially menacing women. No legal assistant gets paid for this kind of adventure." It didn't work. I wanted to be in my bathrobe at home watching *The Lion in Winter*, my bad-mood video, and eating chocolate. A legal assistant could do that every night for a week if she wanted. I gave up on street parking and drove to a garage.

The cocktail lounge was cave-dark, lit only by candles at the tables and the muted pink glow of wall sconces. Sylvia was at a back table, dressed for someone and someplace else. Diamonds glittered on her hands and at her throat. I was relieved to see that she was nursing a glass of mineral water.

"Thank you for meeting me, Maggie. I hope this isn't interfering with your plans for the evening." An image of my chenille bathrobe and a pint of chocolate fudge brownie ice cream flitted through my mind. Probably not what Sylvia meant.

"It's no problem," I said. "But you must have major plans. You look sensational." This wasn't flattery, just a simple statement of fact.

"How sweet of you to say that. Unfortunately it's a rather dreary charity event. The only fun is dressing up for it."

A waiter came by and we both ordered mineral water. Unlike the staff at the Barbary Club, this man didn't fawn over Sylvia. She wasn't a regular here.

"Before we get down to business," I said, "I want to let you know that whoever is following me everywhere is not very good at it, unless they're just out to harass me. Have you spoken with Mr. Ericson about them?"

"I'm sorry, Maggie, I haven't seen Howard since we spoke. I'm afraid I don't understand why they bother you so much, since you're engaged in legal activities, and you're staying at that horrible house. I would think you'd welcome having men 'following you everywhere' for the potential support they offer, in case one of the residents attacks you."

"Be that as it may, they do bother me, and if you and your

husband haven't hired them, I plan to find out who did. I'd be grateful if you could ask him tonight."

"I promise."

"Thanks. Now, how can I help you?"

"Your guess was right. I have met Kelly Henry." Sylvia had an iron grip on that mineral water. Good thing it was thick bar glass and not crystal, or she'd have crushed it.

"The meeting you told me that Kelly missed—it was with you, wasn't it?"

"Yes. I flew in that day to meet her at that horrible house. I brought twenty thousand dollars with me."

"She was blackmailing you."

"Yes, she was." Sylvia shuddered. "It was unbelievably sordid, like living in a *film noir* scene. The fact that the girl is missing just prolongs the agony. I don't know when she'll reappear and make new demands! I had to sell my best piece of jewelry to pay her, and nothing else I own would bring much money."

"Sylvia, I promised that if I could, I'd leave you out of this, but you're an intelligent woman. If something has happened to Kelly Henry, you'll be the first person the police will suspect. If you keep silent about what Kelly was doing, they'll assume—"

"There is no reason why my connection with Ms. Henry needs to be made known in any case."

"What about the airline records of your flight to San Francisco? When you sold your jewelry, that was recorded. And unless you were paid for the jewelry in cash, the bank where you got the money to give Kelly would have a record of that transaction, too. It would be better to give the police everything you know. You may be able to get them to treat it in confidence."

"Thank you, Maggie, for your concern," she said, "I believe that you mean it sincerely. But you cannot possibly know what's involved here. Going to the police with this is out of the question. I do need your help, if you're still willing to work with me on this."

No way was I going to commit myself until I knew more. A lot more.

"What can you tell me about Kelly? What were your impressions of her?"

"Before or after she left my employ?" She noticed my amazement and sighed. "Kelly Henry was employed as temporary domestic help in my home in Phoenix. During the time she worked there, I'm mortified to say that I don't remember her at all, although I must have been in the same room with her a number of times. My housekeeper hired her to do odds and ends, mostly in the kitchen." Sylvia paused for half a minute, swirling the ice in her glass, before she spoke again.

"After she contacted me . . . I have to admit, she frightened me. It was as if she hated me!"

"That must have been very hard to take from someone you had never actually met. Is there anything else you can tell me about her that might be helpful?"

"Well, she must have nerves of steel to risk charges of extortion using the phone and the mail."

"Kelly wrote to you?"

"No, she called me. I couldn't believe this was happening, and I called her bluff, so she mailed me photographs of me having intimate relations with my personal trainer." Sylvia's gaze had been fixed on the fluted shell wall sconce. Now she turned to face me. "It is extremely difficult for me to talk about this. The most intimate part of my life was exposed. The one thing in my life that I had believed was beautiful and true was turned into pornography." She cried silently for a few moments. I handed her a tissue and she dabbed away tears.

"The day I received the photos she called again. She said they were only a small sample. The ones I saw were taken on more than one day. She, or her accomplice, must have been hiding in the walk-in closet. The angle would have been about right from there."

"And she threatened to send them to your husband?"

"You're young, the concept of fidelity may seem absurd to you. But my husband has very traditional ideas about marriage—and the proper role of a wife. He has complete control over my finances. If I ever leave, I take only the clothes on my back. It's in our prenuptial agreement. If Howard saw those photos, he'd divorce me, even though it would break both our hearts."

"What else did Kelly say to you?"

"She told me to bring her the twenty thousand in small bills, and not to even think about going to the police or harming her in any way, because she'd given the photos to someone for safekeeping, and that person would make use of them if anything happened to her."

"Was your trainer involved in the blackmail, do you think?"

"I don't believe he was directly involved. I confronted him when I got the photos. I was close to hysteria. Not long before the photos were taken, Scott persuaded me to 'experiment' with different positions, bondage, costumes. All the photos were from those weeks. That made me suspect that he was mixed up in it somehow. Besides, he was the one who recommended hiring Kelly to my housekeeper. He brought her into my house! But he was so stricken when I accused him . . . He swore he had nothing to do with it, and in the end, I believed him. He's not a scheming type of person."

"Are you still involved with Scott?"

She paused again and chose her words carefully. "Whether or not Scott took part in the blackmail, I knew it was over between us. I haven't seen him for some time."

"I'd like to contact Scott. Would you mind?"

"Why not, if you think it will help?" She recited his number for me.

"Do you have a picture of him I could borrow?"

She pulled a snapshot out of her wallet and laid it facedown on the table. "Here. You don't need to return it."

"Today I learned that Kelly has also used the name Judy. Did you know that?"

"No, but it doesn't surprise me. Nothing about her could surprise me."

"What else can you tell me about her?"

"Sometimes I try to understand why she picked me as her victim. We had never exchanged a word until she contacted me. She insisted that I come to San Francisco and meet her at her house. I was afraid for my life. You've been there, you know what it's like."

It *was* hard to imagine Sylvia walking into that house carrying twenty thousand dollars. She lived in a controlled environment that kept unpleasantness away and anticipated her every need. Under the flattering pink lights, she might have been a sophisticated debutante in her black dinner dress and diamonds. She'd be eaten alive at Capp Street.

"It sounds as if she needed to humiliate you. Do you think that was why she had you come to her house? It's certainly an unlikely thing for a blackmailer to do."

"I believe the humiliation was part of it, but she needed the money."

"Do you remember the date when Kelly first contacted you?"

"August 20. She sent the photos within a week."

"So by the time she contacted you, she was already writing in her journal that Moira was sexually abusing her."

"It's a nightmare."

"Does your husband know that Kelly was employed in your household?"

"Yes, I felt I owed it to him to tell him that much. But he convinced me not to tell Summers."

"Why not?"

"It's one more link to Moira. We were concerned that Summers would refuse to get involved if there were too many pieces of circumstantial evidence against her."

"You won't be able to keep this a secret!"

"Howard will make a few phone calls to the right people, and they'll make sure that nothing comes of it. If Kelly's employment in our home is unrelated to her disappearance, there is no reason for it be made public knowledge."

"Was she after you or Moira—or both of you?"

"I don't see what the connection could be. That's why I need to have you working with me, Maggie, and why I made an offer that you considered inappropriate. I can't pay you much without Howard noticing. All I can promise is to use my connections to help your business. I need your help." She took my hand, and this time I didn't pull away.

"I'll do what I can."

Sylvia pulled a twenty out of her bag and put it next to her glass, and rose gracefully from the table.

"I have faith in you, Maggie." She almost whispered the last words, and left.

A man standing in the shadows of a tree near the door of the lounge looked like Howard Ericson. His hands were poked into his jacket pockets in a way that reminded me of Ericson's posture in his hotel suite the first time we met. I fetched my car from the garage half a block down and drove past the lounge again. The man was gone.

Paranoia, I decided. Hundreds, thousands of men resembled Howard Ericson.

On the drive to Moira's office, I tried to assimilate what I had learned about Kelly that day. It was like a search for several women, with not only different names, but different personalities. The naive victim of the journal, the fragile girl-woman being mauled

112

by Jerry in the Nature's Harmony group picture, the persuasive seller of box seats for the Symphony, the incest survivor, the audacious blackmailer who could dictate whatever terms she chose. Maybe I had been entirely wrong about Moira. Maybe it was the therapist who was the victim here after all.

CHAPTER TWENTY

My short phone conversation with Moira Ericson hadn't prepared me for the woman who answered the doorbell. As she stepped forward to take my hands in hers, I was engulfed in an old-fashioned flowery scent. Her glossy brown curls bounced as she nodded her head and beamed in welcome. Everything about her was rounded, her face, arms, hands. She wore a white turtleneck and matching cardigan with a crystal necklace. A full skirt billowed over her ample hips. The archetype not of a renegade professional but of a suburban matron.

Moira showed me into her spacious, high-ceilinged office. The walls were painted in complementary warm hues, and rugs that might have been Navajo except for their improbable colors were layered on the floor. Through partly shaded French windows I could see a garden. The shelves on one wall were lined with dolls, male and female, newborn to kindergartner.

A term surfaced from Psych 101: I was experiencing "cognitive dissonance." The first few minutes I could do no more than murmur appreciation of color and texture. Gears in my brain were grinding against each other as I adjusted to the sharp difference between the woman I had imagined and the woman showing me around her office.

"I love to watch people's faces when they see all the dolls," she said.

Moira was holding up a red-haired tomboy doll in braids and jeans. "Sometimes our inner child needs some coaxing to come out, and these little ones help. Who wouldn't want to cuddle this one?"

Her mouth-full-of-sugar way of talking struck me now as it had on the phone. Maybe cooing to clients helped them find their inner children by taking them back to when they were unconditionally loved toddlers. It made me want to throw a chair across the room.

Moira picked up a life-sized baby doll wrapped in a pink blanket and held it out to me. "This is everybody's favorite. Would you like to hold her?"

"Oh, no, no thanks." What power we give therapists! I caught myself wondering if I had looked needy, and pulled myself back to business. As my friend Dottie says, when we are out in the adult world, we must leave our inner child safe at home. Especially given present company, even if she could have passed for my Aunt Mildred.

"I have an hour before my next client, and I just made a pot of coffee. Would you like a cup?" I accepted her offer and watched her step into the mini-kitchen to prepare a tray with china, silverware and cloth napkins. Nothing like the drab office with two sagging chairs that my own dyke therapist had occupied. I scanned the room for the couch that could be made into a bed. There was a sofa in the corner of the room that might fold out. I turned away from it with difficulty.

"Thank you for meeting with me," I said. "I know you haven't wanted this investigation."

"No, but since *they* insist on pursuing it, someone from our community might as well benefit from it. How's Tate?" This woman was unbelievably calm. Except for the edge to her voice when she spoke of "them," her tone was unconcerned, even breezy. You'd think we had run into each other at a party. One of us had lost contact with reality.

"Tate is fine, and I'm sure she'd love to see you. Did you know she's been warned away from talking to you?"

"Warned away—what are you talking about?"

"Robert Summers told Tate you didn't want to talk to her or anyone else about what happened with Kelly Henry. That's why I didn't expect that you would see me."

"I don't want to see my father or that woman he married, and they're the ones who hired the attorney, Summers, so naturally I have no interest in dealing with him. Mr. Summers kept badgering me to give him the names of other therapists I'd worked with. Tate was one of them. I guess he took my refusal to speak with him and my father as extending to everyone else."

"Tell me about Kelly Henry."

"You know I can't tell you much, because of my duty of confidentiality."

"But surely, given her disappearance, the limits of confidentiality would change—"

"My limits aren't necessarily the ones imposed by law. Kelly has not terminated therapy with me. I won't jeopardize her being able to return to therapy just because it would be more convenient for others if I violated her trust."

"Did you start seeing Kelly at the Therapy Center, then tell her to lie about continuing to see you?" The devil made me want to take a poke at her self-righteous posture.

She smiled serenely and spread her hands in front of her, palms up. "I can see how it looks now, out of context. But the truth is, the Center's operating grant puts dozens of stupid bureaucratic restrictions on what we can do. Everybody breaks the rules, and everyone knows it, but it's all unspoken. Until, of course, something like this happens."

"Has anything 'like this' ever happened before?"

"No, Maggie, that was a figure of speech."

"Okay. You started seeing her here on June 19?"

"I'd have to check my book, but that sounds about right." She stepped to her desk and picked up a massive leather appointment book. While she leafed through its pages, I glanced around the room, and heard myself draw a sudden breath when I saw a tall free-standing mirror on a swivel. I imagined Kelly naked, reluctantly caressing herself, with Moira guiding her hands. When Moira sat down next to me I flinched, and had to resist the urge to move away from her.

"Yes, it was the 19th," she said, watching me as if I were a potential client who was too far gone for outpatient therapy. "Are you all right?"

"I'm fine, thanks. Can you tell me Kelly's diagnosis?"

"First of all, I don't see my clients as walking sets of symptoms. Each one is an individual, experiencing problems with real-life situations. But in any case, that's confidential. And we're getting into the area that made me tell my father and his attorney to stay away."

"What else *can* you tell me?"

"Just that I saw her two, sometimes three times a week, at her insistence, until the day she went missing."

"Did she ask you questions about your family?"

"I don't remember anything that seemed inappropriate. I share more of my life than many therapists do. I don't believe in coming across like the Great and Powerful Wizard of Oz behind the curtain. For example, I don't respond the way some therapists would to a question about my own mother." She nodded again. I diagnosed an approval-giving technique that had become habitual.

"Would you have answered her questions?"

"Typically I would have attempted to find out what was the question behind her question—what she was trying to explore about her relationship with her own mother."

117

"But you answered personal questions that Kelly asked you?"

"Yes. The same way that I am answering your personal questions now."

Her voice had risen in anger when she answered. A hairline crack in her poise that immediately was sealed up again. We drank our coffee in silence for a minute.

"Do you ever touch your clients?"

She chuckled in response. "Ah, the old physical contact debate. Well, I might hug them when they arrive or when they leave, and when someone gets an AA chip or achieves some other milestone, I might spontaneously put my arms around them. Why?"

"Because Kelly alleges that you touched her a great deal. Have you ever had sex with a client?"

"That's unethical, although I've heard stories, of course. Is it important to *you* for sexuality not to be an issue in therapy, Maggie?" I thought momentarily of my massive, and unacknowledged, crush on my own therapist, then pushed the memory aside.

"I think it's important for everyone to be safe in therapy. Do you know what Kelly says about you in her journal?"

"No. The police were upset about it, and my father's lawyer wanted me to read a photocopy of it. But as I said, I need to be available to Kelly if she comes back, and reading her private journal would violate her trust."

"Moira, she says you made her your slave, completely dependent on you. She says you made her clean your house in return for therapy that consisted of you abusing her sexually! Doesn't this concern you?"

"You identify with her very deeply, don't you?" she said thoughtfully, and very slowly moved her head up and down.

I pushed on: "I'd like to track down a couple of visitors Kelly had in her room. One was a white man, a body-builder type.

Any idea who that might have been?"

"Surely you know that I can't talk about the content of our sessions. That's what makes me ask myself what you really came here for."

Moira reminded me of an assistant D.A. who had cross-examined me about my surveillance report in a trial a few weeks earlier. Although their styles were altogether different, both were used to running the show, and no matter what you said, their method was to shape the interaction in a way that kept them in control. The D.A. couldn't shake my testimony, and I had no intention of letting this woman sidetrack me.

"Okay, we'll leave content aside. Did Kelly ever come to your home?"

Moira was silent for almost a minute. She took a careful sip of coffee, gently lowered the cup to its saucer and met my eyes.

"She was in my house once, but I noticed her in my neighborhood a couple of times before that. I thought about bringing it up to her but never did. Now I think she must have been watching me for awhile. I also saw her near my office when I left for the day on several occasions, and these were days we didn't have a session."

"Do you think she might have been stalking you?"

"Stalking? Like the movie stars that have obsessive fans following them?"

"Exactly."

"I wouldn't have thought so. There's nothing mysterious about me, nothing to feed the obsessions of a stalker."

"What happened the time she came to your house?"

"She said she was desperate, she had to see me, that it couldn't wait until our next session, which was four days away."

"What did you do?"

"She was extremely upset. I was concerned that she might be suicidal. She refused to go to the crisis center, so I phoned the

M.D. I work with when a client needs medication, and arranged to have him call in a prescription for her, to calm her down. I gave her a cup of tea, and when she was ready I called a cab for her, and sent her home."

"If she went home, how did she get the prescription?"

"The cab driver waited for her at the pharmacy, then took her home. I don't see what difference it makes now."

"It might make a considerable difference if you can give an explanation, and produce witnesses, for how Kelly knew details of what your house looks like. How much of your place did she see?"

"Everything except the bedroom. She used the bathroom and I served her the tea in the kitchen."

"Did you leave her alone at any time?"

"No, I—wait, I had been taking a bath when she rang my doorbell, and I went back into the bathroom. She would have had ten minutes to herself then. I remember worrying that she would use one of my kitchen knives on herself."

"And that was the only time she was ever inside your house?"

"You don't want to believe me, do you? And it's so much harder for you, now that you've met me." Moira shook her head, smiling sadly.

Rising somewhat unsteadily from my chair, I thanked her for her time and the coffee, and left with my dignity in shreds. Then I remembered an important question I hadn't asked, and went back. "Just one more thing," I said. "Did you know her real name was Judy?"

"She used a false name with me?" Moira shook her head dazedly, as if she'd been punched and was trying to clear her vision.

"So, you didn't know?"

"No. Why would Kelly lie to me?"

While I drove away I kept glancing back at Moira standing in

120

the lighted doorway, that stricken look fixed on her face. Funny, I'd have thought that pulling a Lieutenant Columbo, getting in the last word, would have been more satisfying.

CHAPTER TWENTY-ONE

I parked a block over from Capp Street and looked around casually for surveillance as I neared the house. A bunch of men who were passing around a bottle in a paper bag gave me their full attention at the corner. Several of them crooned endearments in English and Spanish. It was unlikely that they were there on anyone's payroll. The smallest of the group sprang in front of me. "Hey, *mami*, what's your hurry, don't you like us?"

"I'm sure you're a great bunch of guys, but I've had a long day. Bye." I lengthened my stride. He had to take two steps for each of mine, but he kept up.

"I'll take you to your door, *mami*. There's some *vatos locos* around here, you know?"

"Thanks. Good night. I'm sure you'll meet somebody nice tonight." Winded from race-walking, I shot inside and almost collided with the dreadlocked scavenger. The smell emanating from him was especially pungent tonight. He rocked backward as if I might hit him.

"Good evening," I said.

His mouth hung open for a few seconds. "Evening," he grunted, and fled down the hall, dragging a burlap sack full of bottles noisily behind him.

I stopped at Lisa's door but there was no response to my knock. I stood there for a minute until I made out sounds of a man in the final throes of orgasm, sighed and continued to my room without running into any other tenants.

The room felt terribly empty. I missed Liam and the animals. The pay phone in the hall rang, I counted, seven times. I opened the door and looked around. Nobody. I picked up the receiver and said hello.

"Kelly?" a man responded cautiously.

"No, I'm trying to find her myself—" The caller hung up halfway through my last words.

Since I was already at the phone, I called home for messages. Liam greeted me groggily. On the periphery of my vision a small creature scuttled along the wall. I half-listened to Liam tell about the latest interdepartmental feud at his job and how much he missed Sam as I watched it dart into a hole. Surely it was a mouse. But the tail was long enough to belong to a small rat.

Liam's whoop brought me back. "Maggie, I forgot! There's a message for you from somebody named Leslie. She wanted to know who exactly I was, and what my relationship was to you, before she'd talk to me. I said I was your assistant."

"That works for me."

"It worked for her, too, so she told me that Judy's last name is Simmons. She also told me that calling other Program people like that made her feel unclean, and *she* could never stand to do the kind of work 'you people' do for a living. I wanted to thank her for sharing, but I didn't, since I was impersonating a representative of the firm of Windsor & Garrett, not to mention that I'm a guest in your house."

"Thanks, you're a prince. What are you up to, tonight?"

"I wouldn't blame you if you tried to talk me out of doing this, but I'm meeting Sam for coffee. We both think we need to talk some more to get closure. You think it's a mistake, don't you?"

"No, closure is good." I was trying to remember why I should be adamantly opposed to their talking when a crash of splintering wood came from the end of the hall, followed by a duet for two screamers, the principal lyrics of which were "mine" and "was not." A baby wailed furiously downstairs, and someone turned the volume of a Spanish-language TV program to the maximum.

"Maggie, are you all right? What's all that noise?"

"Just a quiet evening at home. Don't worry, I'm fine."

"I think I should come over and stay with you. If all those heterosexuals know you're by yourself—you know how obsessed with sex they are . . . ." The mouse/rat ran back into the hall, halted in its tracks and stared at me cheekily. By tomorrow it would be demanding Fancy Feast.

"I'll be fine, honest. I even have a pet. Besides, I've got my .38. If the bad guys broke down the door and you were with me, I'd probably end up shooting you! Have a good time tonight."

"Maggie, we are *not* getting together for the fun of it."

"Sorry, have a good closure."

I called Ricardo and told him Kelly/Judy's last name so he could get going. He was hot for the challenge, and I knew he'd keep going until he got what we needed. Too bad his high school classes couldn't motivate him that way.

Back in my room, I changed from my client drag into sweats and tried to get comfortable on the lumpy mattress. I turned the radio volume way up. John Coltrane drowned out two women shrieking invectives in Spanish. "Everything's going to fall into place tomorrow," I promised myself, and picked up a Joseph Hansen mystery. It was going to be a long night.

Something crawled over my face and I woke up with a start. The overhead light was still on. I'd fallen asleep reading. Had the crawly sensation been the tickle of a spider or roach or the brush of rat tail? Shuddering, I shook out the covers and looked under the bed. The fact that I didn't find anything was not a comfort. There was a spider in the corner of the room, but it was occupied with a fly.

I was now fully awake at 3:05 A.M.—the worst time. Too early to get up, and too few hours left to really get back into the groove of sleeping before I had to be up and functional. I picked up the Joseph Hansen, but even Dave Brandstetter couldn't hold my attention.

My mind kept wandering to the sealed room down the hall. From what Summers, the Ericsons' attorney, had told me, as well as from Al's complaints, I suspected that the police search of Kelly's room had been perfunctory. There might be something, a scrap of paper left in a pocket, a photo of a friend, that would give me a lead. Everything I learned through other people was later contradicted by some other, equally believable source. I needed something tangible, not filtered through other people's interpretations.

No doubt about it, I had to break into her room. If I was going to do it, now was the ideal time. I pulled on a dark sweatshirt with a kangaroo pocket in front and soft canvas slip-on shoes. I put my flashlight and an extremely unofficial set of picklocks in the pocket of my sweatpants, and my .38 in the kangaroo pocket. The crowbar I'd brought to the house for a weapon felt reassuringly solid under my arm. I opened the door.

The hallway was dark. Did that cheap sleaze Al turn out the lights at night? I pointed the flashlight at the light fixture. The bulb was gone.

I padlocked my door and moved down the hall as quietly as the creaky old floorboards allowed. No lights showed under any of the other doors off the hall.

Kelly's room had been sealed with police tape, and an SFPD notice of a pending investigation was stuck on the door with some kind of adhesive. Nearly all the tape had been peeled off, and graffiti covered the notice. A heavy board had been nailed across the door.

It is very difficult to pry a board off two-inch nails in silence, in the dark. Every few minutes I panned the beam of the flashlight over the area. Once there was a skittering noise near my foot and I nearly dropped the crowbar. My heart was thumping somewhere in the vicinity of my throat. The last nail slipped out of the wood more easily than I expected and the board fell to the floor with a muffled thump. The muffling was provided by my foot.

I stood still in the darkness for a couple of minutes, waiting for the pain to subside and listening for any response in the hall. Nothing. I pulled on latex gloves and attacked the padlock. It was a breeze compared to the board, even though I rarely use the picks and will never surpass talented amateur status with them.

The door creaked dramatically when I opened it. I closed it quickly and waited again for any sound from the hallway. Finally I couldn't stand the suspense any longer.

I switched on the flashlight and waved it around the room. My hopes for revealing bits of information from Kelly's possessions were dashed. The room was almost empty. No pictures hung on the walls. The surfaces of the room were bare: no souvenirs, books or even empty dishes. The contents of a chest in the corner had been tossed. All the drawers were pulled out, and articles of clothing dangled over the sides of the drawers. The sheets and coverlet on the bed had been rucked up when investigators checked the mattress.

I turned on the overhead light to free up my hands. There was a simple latch hook on the door and I fastened it shut. I stuffed a bed sheet around the bottom of the door to keep light from showing in the dark hallway. The fabric of the sheet wasn't the cheap stuff I expected, and I looked at it more closely. It was a rather unpleasant shade of green, but the fabric was fine linen. I recognized the name of the maker from a short security stint at a posh Union Street bedding boutique. A sheet like this could cost hundreds of dollars.

The other sheet and comforter cover were made of the same fabric, although the comforter itself was the kind you can buy for ten bucks from vendors in the Mission District. My guess was that Kelly had stolen the bedding from the Ericsons while she was working for them. If this were true, it would give Kelly a reason to bring Sylvia here: to flaunt proof that she'd had access to Sylvia's bedroom. Of course, it might also have belonged to Moira, but the color seemed closer to Sylvia's taste than Moira's.

A stained polyester-filled pillow lay on the floor. I wondered why there was no pillow slip. If the police had been as intrigued by the bedding as I, maybe they had taken it for analysis.

The closet contained an ancient pea-coat with a MUNI FastPass for the month before and forty-three cents in its pockets, a couple of ancient sweatshirts, nondescript blouses, pants and skirts, and a soft cardigan sweater that bore a label from a San Francisco store that sold only Scottish cashmeres. It was similar in style and size to the one Moira had worn earlier in the evening.

Could Moira have given the sweater to her, or was it stolen too? How could the police have missed this? Radar for designer labels and luxury fibers was a strong argument for recruiting more gay men and femmes to the SFPD.

Next, the chest. Kelly hadn't helped herself to anyone's lingerie. There were a few pairs of cotton underpants, several T-shirts, two pairs of jeans. I looked behind the drawers and behind the chest as the police must have done before me. Nothing.

I had crawled under the bed to look for hiding places under the box springs when I heard the door knob turn. The door pushed against the latch tentatively and then with some force. I scrambled to my feet and picked up the .38.

If by bizarre chance it was the police out there, I was in trouble. If it was any number of other people out there, I was in a different kind of trouble. The flimsy latch wouldn't keep anyone out for long.

I moved close to the door, kicked the sheet out of the way and assumed a shooter's stance. "Who is it?" I whispered hoarsely.

There was no response. I thought I heard steps moving away.

Okay, I told myself, let's not be overly dramatic here. Most likely it was someone on the way to the toilet down the hall. He'd noticed that the board was off Kelly's door and was hoping to steal something from the room. Yeah, he was probably the same guy who stole the light bulb from the hallway! He went away as soon as he heard my voice. He wouldn't call the cops. Not even murders got reported in a place like this.

I counted to three hundred, then restored the room to the same disorder as before. I decided to lock the padlock again and take the board with me. I couldn't nail it back on without making a lot of noise. Besides, if tenants were stealing lightbulbs, why not boards?

I opened the door and arced the flashlight beam around the hallway. No one in sight. I stuck the .38 back in the sweatshirt pocket and turned to close the padlock.

I heard rapid footsteps, then a whooshing sound. A hand roughly grasped my wrist, and the flashlight fell to the floor with a clatter.

"What you lookin' for in there?" The intense body odor told me that it was the dreadlocked scavenger who didn't like to have his face seen.

"I'm trying to find Kelly. I thought maybe I'd find something in there that could help her."

"Too late." He let go of my wrist and turned away.

"Wait, what do you mean?" I picked up the flashlight and shined it in his general direction, but away from his face.

"Big woman hurt her."

"What did this woman look like?"

"Big, rich. Evil woman." He walked away slowly, with a heavy tread.

Back in my room, I finished the bottled mineral water I'd brought to the room after I got a close look at what came out of the bathroom sink. Had anything become clearer through my late-night breaking and entering? I lay down on the bed in the dark, closed my eyes to help me concentrate better, and immediately fell asleep.

CHAPTER TWENTY-TWO

The grinding and crashing noises that accompany Sunset Scavengers' rounds woke me at five A.M. I thrashed about for another hour before concluding that another minute on that bed was out of the question. Somewhere there were firm, supportive mattresses that didn't stink. Somewhere there were hot showers and good coffee. I threw on jeans and T-shirt and bolted for the car.

The forced wakefulness of driving made me think about the scavenger's words the night before. A big woman had hurt Kelly, he said. Should I take him seriously? Sometimes it seemed as if thousands of people were staggering around San Francisco talking to themselves and kicking trees, many of whom could be functional if they got their mental sparkplugs changed once in a while. The scavenger most likely was one of those people. Still, I suspected that he had seen *something*.

The aroma of Spinelli's Mocha Java met me when I opened the door of my cottage—Liam had finally mastered the overnight timer. I looked over at the couch to see if he was stirring yet, and saw two sleeping forms under a quilt on the floor. It appeared that closure was not what Liam and Sam had achieved the night before.

After a shower and two cups of coffee, I was ready to consider my next move. Another report was due to Summers. This was not a big deal, but I had to decide what, if anything, to report about my trip into Kelly's room, then phone each of the Ericsons before delivering the written report. That was a big deal.

Sam came into the kitchen. "Hi, Mags." He is the only one who has ever called me this. I try not to mind.

"How are you, Sam?"

"Stiff!" He rolled his head and his shoulders popped. "It's a little unusual to be camping on somebody else's floor when you have an apartment with a queen-size bed in it, but Liam felt more comfortable staying here."

"Coffee?"

"Sure."

Until I talked to Liam, I didn't feel like being cozy with Sam. We drank our coffee in silence. I fed the animals, took Pugsley for a short run, then dressed in a marginally passable jacket, blouse and slacks, in case I was obliged to see the Ericsons in person.

Fifteen feet from my office door I felt the vibrations emanating from the Windsor & Garrett boombox. Ricardo was already at work. I'd be getting another complaint from the accountant next door, who had been sleeping in his office since his wife kicked him out. The low level of coffee in the pot indicated that Ricardo had been there for hours. He greeted me with a grin of accomplishment.

"We're closing in on Judy Simmons, boss. I've just got to make a couple more calls . . . ."

"That's fantastic, but none of the places we need to call will be open for another hour, by which time you have to be in class. Make a list and I'll call them."

"But Maggie—"

"I know it's hard to delegate, and nobody else could do it as well as you do. But I promise I'll make you proud. Go get yourself some breakfast." I stuck a fiver in his hand and pushed him out the door.

The first call was to Ricardo's cousin Ubaldo at the Department of Motor Vehicles. After he grumbled indignantly over my using "Rico's" name to get information, Ubaldo confirmed that Judy Simmons matched Kelly's description and approximate age. Six years earlier she had been issued a California ID, but not a driver's license, in Sunnyvale. I got the home address, and through directory assistance confirmed that there was a Rupert Simmons listed at 2857 Farm Glen Drive.

Before I set off to visit the Simmons family, it was worth trying to reach Sylvia's trainer/ex-lover Scott Bentley. It was still only a little after nine o'clock in Phoenix. He might still be at home. I dialed the number Sylvia had given me. An elderly-sounding woman answered, with a rich twang in her voice. When I asked for Scott Bentley, she hooted. "Bentley! His name's Scotty Hogg. It was good enough back in Fort Worth." She half covered the receiver and yelled "Scotteee!" I heard a growled male response in the background and, half-muffled, "Well, how the heck would I know who it is—some girl!" She returned to me: "He'll be right here. Bentley," she muttered, "how in blazes did he come up with that one?"

Angry rumbles grew in volume as Scott approached the phone. He continued to quiz the elderly woman about who was calling and what exactly she had told me.

"Yes? This is Scott." He spoke unaccented TV-announcer English in a rich bass–baritone.

"Hello, Mr. Bentley, my name is Maggie Garrett. I'm a private investigator working for Sylvia Ericson. She gave me your phone number."

"Listen, I don't know how Kelly got the pictures." Panic made his voice go up an octave, and the old woman's Texas twang took over. "I've told Sylvia a hundred times I didn't have anything to do with it. Working for Sylvia was a cinch. Why would I blow it by setting her up?" I could hear the woman asking questions in the background, with Bentley/Hogg trying unsuccessfully to put her off.

"Mr. Bentley, that's not why I'm calling you. The Ericsons have hired me to find the woman you knew as Kelly Henry. Her real name is Judy Simmons, but I'm used to calling her Kelly by now. Is that okay with you?"

"Are they pressing charges on the photos?" He sounded even more scared.

"Relax, Mr. Bentley, no one has mentioned prosecuting you . . . Kelly was reported missing three weeks ago, and the police questioned Mr. Ericson's daughter Moira about it. The Ericsons hired me to find Kelly so that Moira wouldn't be suspected of doing her any harm."

"Moira? What does she have to do with Kelly?"

"You know both of these women?"

"Well, I don't *know* Moira, but one time when I was in San Francisco with Sylvia we ran into her. I was underwhelmed, and of course she and Sylvia hate each other, so neither of the ladies was at her best. And I know Kelly, or Judy, whatever the hell her name really turns out to be. What a nightmare! I thought she was this little kid who had run away from home. She told me her parents had given her uncle custody of her, and that he tried to molest her. So she said she had to hide out, otherwise he'd take her back. She had me completely fooled."

"You don't think what she told you was true?"

"I don't know. You're telling me she wasn't who she said she was. Anyway, after what she did to me with those pictures, I wouldn't believe anything she said."

"How did you meet her?"

"Hold on a minute." He covered the phone but his voice came through. "Ma, here's fifty bucks. Go get some groceries! Get whatever you want, I don't care. Hi, I'm back. Kelly and I went to several of the same Narcotics Anonymous meetings, and we got to know each other."

"Did you get the impression that Kelly did drugs?"

"I'm not supposed to tell you because of anonymity, but I don't think she had ever used drugs. First I thought she was really dedicated to her recovery. See, in a place like San Francisco, there's a meeting for any kind of addiction, at any hour, all kinds of places. We don't have that many meetings here, so you make do sometimes to get to a 12-step program. She came to one of my Sex and Love Addicts Anonymous meetings, and I saw her come out of an Overeaters Anonymous meeting one time."

"So she could work the steps with other Program people?"

"You in the Program?"

"No but I had a lover who was. She used to say that, in a pinch, any 12-step group could work. I went to a whole variety of meetings with her when we were traveling."

"Well, you hit it, that was exactly what Kelly told me, that she was having trouble with the Fourth Step, and it didn't matter what the addiction was, it helped to be around 12-step people. Most of the groups meet at the same church, so she spent a lot of time hanging out there. But Kelly would act like a different person in these meetings."

"How was she different?"

"She'd share in an NA meeting, and she'd make you think she'd been using since she was ten, but she didn't talk about relationships or eating. In the SLAA meeting she never mentioned drugs or food. And that time I followed her out of a building where she'd been to OA, she was talking to a couple of girls from the meeting, and she sounded like she was just powerless over food. I decided she was a meeting junkie. You meet them sometimes. They need the meetings like they used to need their drugs or booze. I began to think she was one of those people—nutty, but not in a bad way. When you're a new person in those meetings, you get a lot of positive energy from people."

"Did you see her outside of the meetings?"

"We'd go for coffee . . . a whole bunch of us did every week, after the Saturday night meeting. After a few weeks she asked me if I'd be her sponsor. I told her I couldn't, because I'm a man and she's a woman. But after she asked me, it made me look at her differently. I sort of felt responsible for her after that."

"Were you involved with her sexually?"

"You've got a lot of nerve . . ."

"It's my job. Should I assume the answer is yes and you're being an old-fashioned gentleman?"

"God, no, she was like a little kid, a runaway. Look, I don't know how much Sylvia told you about me . . . ."

"Not very much, but I've seen a snapshot of you and I know that you're very attractive."

"Thanks. My body and my face, that's all I've got. I dropped out of junior college. Training these rich women, letting them show me off to their friends, sometimes even having a friendly roll in the hay—that's all part of the job, and I'm good at it."

"And you don't date girls who have even less money than you do . . . ." I bet you don't date women at all if you're not paid for it, I added silently.

"Well, that's a crude way of putting it, but yeah. My ladies wouldn't like seeing me with a girl her age. Let's face it, the older woman-younger man fantasy has a whole lot to do with me getting work. And once in a while they want more than a fantasy, they want safe sex. In other words, if I'm safe, they don't have to use anything. So if I was messing around, especially with a street kid, they'd drop me fast."

"Maybe you can help me out with what Sylvia told me. I don't understand how someone you met in 12-step groups ended up getting into Sylvia's house to take pictures of you."

"That's no secret. I brought her there. See, Sylvia has a twenty-room house, and there's never enough people to do all the work, even with a live-in housekeeper and cook, and a bunch of guys who come in and take care of the heavy work. Last fall Sylvia and Howard threw a major party, and they brought in outside help for it. I told Sylvia's housekeeper I knew a girl who'd work cheap. That's how Kelly got into the house."

"Only that once?"

"No, she was there all during the holidays, and then maybe a dozen times after that. The housekeeper got to keep the money she saved on an agency, so she kept calling Kelly back."

"Do you know anything about where Kelly was living in Phoenix, or how she was supporting herself when she wasn't working for Sylvia Ericson?"

There was a profound silence on the other end. Finally Scott said, "I have no idea. She didn't talk about that kind of thing, now that you mention it. I guess I never thought about it before."

"How did Kelly find out about you and Sylvia? Did you tell her?"

"I didn't need to. Sylvia—I don't know how to put this . . . She went over the edge about us. Sometimes she'd forget there was anybody else in the house, and say things, or put her hands on me. The staff used to gossip about us."

"Sylvia's terrified that her husband will find out about the two of you. It doesn't make sense that she could have been so careless about the household help seeing the two of you, and then so nervous about the photos."

"Like I told you, she went over the edge a little bit—"

"She was in love with you," I said. I was losing patience with him. "Did she believe that you were in love with her?"

"It's none of your business!"

"Would you rather talk to me or the police?" I waited. Finally he spoke.

"Well, yeah, I guess you could say that. She had this idea that we were going to run off someplace together. Listen, I was Sylvia's trainer for a year and a half. It paid better than any gig I'd ever had. Then she got it into her head that me doing a good job boffing her was the same thing as wanting to, like, marry her. What was I supposed to do? Say, 'Gee, sorry, Mrs. Ericson, but you're twenty-five years older than me, and you've had too much liposuction'?"

"Not to mention that you found out she didn't have any money of her own?"

"I don't have to answer that. I'm hanging up now."

"You hang up, and I'm calling Missing Persons with a hot tip about Kelly Henry's disappearance."

"You're really a bitch."

"Thanks. So Sylvia was careless about the staff knowing about you because she thought the two of you were going to elope, until it all fell apart. How about Howard? Do you know him very well?"

"The whole time I worked for Sylvia I don't think I saw Howard ten times, which was fine with me. He didn't like me, to put it mildly. He's got all the finesse of a wild boar, and he always made fun of me for being a trainer."

Then there was the fact that you were boffing his wife.

"Did he strike you as a possessive husband? Would he be vindictive if he found out his wife was unfaithful?"

"I don't know. The man lives to work. He has no idea what Sylvia does during the twenty-three hours a day that he doesn't see her. I don't think they sleep together much anymore. Of course that doesn't mean he wouldn't care about her doing it with somebody else."

"Angry enough to do more than take away her charge cards?"

"Like get violent? I don't know, he's awfully intense. I guess it's a possibility. What's all this got to do with Kelly?"

"Background. I'm trying to find out how Kelly knew that Sylvia would pay big money to keep Howard from seeing those pictures. Did you ever talk to her about Howard and Sylvia?"

"Sure, once in awhile, I guess. Are you saying he might come after me?" The panic had returned to his voice.

"No, I was thinking that he might go after Kelly, since she's the one holding the photos—and the negatives. When did you find out about the photos?"

"Sylvia called me in the middle of the night. She had just gotten the pictures in the mail. It was wild, I had a, um, friend staying over and Sylvia was screaming. To tell the truth, it was more like wailing, you know, the way women carry on at funerals? I remember she was so loud my friend could hear every word. It was embarrassing! I had to take the phone outside and sit on the front step. Sylvia isn't the kind of woman who falls apart. But that night she was out of control. She kept asking over and over who was this Kelly, was she my girlfriend, why had I let her down? As if *I* had taken the damned pictures!"

"This was the end of August?"

"Yeah."

"Do you have any idea where Kelly would go if she left San Francisco in a hurry? I'm worried about her."

"No, but you can bet it isn't me she'd come to. After she messed up things with Sylvia, she'd have to know she couldn't sucker me again."

"When was the last time you saw her?"

"You mean here?" A gasp followed this, as he scrambled for a way to take back his words. "I, uh, I mean the last time she was here that I would've seen her was, I guess, sometime in July. But I'm not sure, don't quote me."

"I've got a couple more questions that may sound weird, but bear with me."

"Okay." He seemed relieved that I hadn't pressed him about where he last saw Kelly.

"What kind of sheets do the Ericsons have in their bedroom?"

"*Sheets?*"

"Yeah, are they some special kind?"

"Um, it's a French name, I ought to know it. Anyway they're linen. Sylvia got this antique wallpaper stuff, so she had the sheets made up in a custom color to match it."

"Are they green?"

"Yeah, why?"

"I told you they were weird questions. Number two: Do you remember Kelly having a gray cashmere sweater?"

"That's a joke, right?"

"I'll take that as a no. Do you know the names of any of her friends?"

"I don't think she had any, just people she sat next to in meetings. One time she told me I was her best friend. Makes you wonder, huh?"

CHAPTER TWENTY-THREE

Howard Ericson started yelling at me the moment I picked up the phone. "What's this nonsense about you being followed? And where do you get off calling my wife and grilling her? I thought we had an agreement that you talk directly with me!"

"First of all, that call didn't relate to your private matters, and second, neither of our agreements involved you having me shadowed! I know that you fired the Glass Agency. So it makes sense to suspect that you hired a new set of goons."

"I am not having you followed, and my arrangements with Glass or any other contractors are none of your business. What I do outside our employment relationship is no concern of yours."

"So you deny hiring the Parker Agency?"

"I have to say I am dissatisfied with your work product so far, Ms. Garrett. I will be even more dissatisfied if I discover that I am being billed for the time you spend on neurotic suspicions about being followed. Have you got anything new to report?"

I told him that Kelly was in fact Judy Simmons, and that I was planning to visit her parents. I also gave him a highly edited version of my conversation with Scott. I omitted my middle of the night trip to Judy's room.

"It was that faggot Scott," he spat the name, "who brought her into my house."

"Yes, he told me, but it seems to have been from honest

motives."

"Hah! You should've seen the lisping pantywaist that he wanted my wife to hire as a driver—"

"I *do* bill at triple rates for listening to offensive language, Mr. Ericson!"

"Oh, right. Sorry," Howard growled. "Anyway, forget about guys following you. You'd do better to look further into what that fa—to look into what Scott was up to."

"Is there any way you might have met Judy when she was working in your home?"

"Unlikely. I stay out of running the household. Sorry, Ms. Garrett, I always lose my temper talking to you. I'm sure you know your business. Just do what you can for my Moira. It's possible Bentley is telling the truth . . . somebody isn't, that's for sure. Keep me apprised!" He hung up.

I relaxed my jaw, which had developed a tic of clenching whenever I spoke to Howard Ericson. If I was going to exercise this much self-censorship, I might as well join the Diplomatic Corps. And I was stuck with my spooks. Howard Ericson disclaimed them and Sylvia suggested that I consider them my personal bodyguards. I jogged to the garage to work off my frustration and frustrate any followers.

The Toyota had been acting up lately. Its drug-dealing former owner had done a lot of custom work to its innards, so it has a lot more power than when it came off the assembly line. Spike, the head mechanic at Labyris Wymmin's Wheels, believes that such tampering with the automotive version of Mother Nature accelerates a car's aging process. In other words, "Live hard, die young." Every time I bring in the car, Spike counsels me to prepare for its imminent demise. This made me a little nervous about driving on the freeway for forty miles, but the Toyota was my only option. The van is only good for stationary surveillance in comfort and anonymity.

I stopped off at home to grab some cassettes and to kidnap Pugsley for company. He barked warnings at dogs in other cars and woofed along as I sang back-up harmonies to an old Pixies tape.

An hour later we were in a lower-middle-class neighborhood in Sunnyvale. There were almost no cars on the street, and I was able to park in front of the Simmons' house. It was identical to those around it, except that the area that was covered by sod or flowers in other yards was covered by pea green cement in this one.

A ceramic sign above the doorbell of the house admonished me that THE WAGES OF SIN IS DEATH. I often saw similar signs growing up in Iowa. Their effect was to throw me into grammatical confusion rather than fear for my immortal soul.

I rang the doorbell several times before a woman's face appeared in the small pane in the door. She squinted at me through the window and waved her hand in dismissal, most likely summing me up as a magazine seller or canvasser. I held up my P.I. license. If you don't know better, it looks intimidating. She put her face against the glass to peer at the license, and then at my face again. Ostentatiously hooking the chain lock on the door, she opened it a crack. The woman's head was covered with home-permanent rods and her upper body was draped in a plastic table cloth that crackled with every movement.

"Mrs. Rupert Simmons?" Her only response was a stony glare. "My name is Maggie Garrett. I'm a private investigator, and I'm looking for Judy Simmons' mother. Is that you?"

She moved her head in assent very slightly. "What do you want?" Her features were set in an expression of pained disappointment, and the words seemed to force themselves out of her mouth, against her will.

"Judy has been missing from her home and her job in San Francisco for over three weeks." The woman's hand gripped the side of the door, hard. "May I come in and talk to you?"

"No." She moved to bar the door as if I might try to push past her. "A lady from my church is here, giving me this permanent, and she doesn't need to know my family's private business." She stepped outside and pulled the door shut behind her. "If Judy's in trouble again, she's on her own. She's been 'missing' from this home for two years. The girl is not our daughter anymore, we washed our hands of her."

"How long has it been since you had any contact with Judy?"

"Over a year, I guess. Last time she called, my husband answered, and he told her it was the Lord she'd better ask for help, not us. We haven't heard from her since." Her voice lacked conviction. I wondered how things might have turned out if she had taken that call instead of her husband.

"You asked if she's in trouble *again?* What kind of trouble did she get into before?"

"She'd get herself in a mess somewhere and need to have money sent to her. My husband said she was running with Satan. One time she got beaten up in Chicago—I never did hear the details." Her mouth worked as she relived the incident. "My husband wouldn't let me go see her, said she brought it on herself. God willing, she'll learn something from it, he said."

"Do you have any idea why she might be using an assumed name?"

"No."

"Do you have other children, Mrs. Simmons?" Her face tightened in pain.

"I bore two daughters. The oldest one took her own life rather than forsake the devil's path."

"I'm so sorry. Losing a daughter that way must have been so painful."

"My husband said it was God's will. I pray to the Lord every night, asking what I've done to make both my daughters turn away from His path."

"I'm not much of a churchgoer anymore, but I was raised with the idea of redemption and forgiveness. Maybe Judy will find her way back."

"My husband would never allow that. He cast her out. After he found out about Wendy's unnatural ways, he looked to find the same weakness in Judy. He even went around talking to her friends, asking them did they lie down together in a way that was against Bible teaching? Marnie Durman's dad came over and threatened to beat him up if he ever talked to Marnie again." She poked absently at the curling rods in her hair.

"Wendy was a lesbian?"

"I won't hear that word!" She recoiled as if I had slapped her. "A woman who could go against God's plan that way is nothing but a sinner and a fornicator."

"But why did your husband think both girls would, uh, turn out that way? There's no proof that it runs in families."

"He said it was a trial of his faith, and that he had to cast out both his daughters to show the Lord the strength of his faithfulness." There was bitterness in her voice when she said "*his* daughters."

"But you're still grieving for Wendy, and you still care about Judy. I know my mother would love me whatever happened with me, whether she understood it or not, and I think that's the essence of Christian love."

"That's as may be. It's not our way."

"When I was growing up in Iowa, I used to hear people talk about what they would do to get the devil to leave someone who was possessed. Did your husband try any other ways to keep the girls from going bad, besides praying for them?

"Why are you asking about my husband?"

How did you ask a woman whether her husband abused or molested his daughters?

"I'm trying to get a complete picture of Judy, and our families know us best, don't you think?"

"He was a hard father, but a righteous one. He locked Wendy in her room so she couldn't be influenced by that daughter of Satan again."

"Who was the other girl?"

"It was her that led Wendy off the godly path."

"Do you know her name, or what happened to her?"

"No. The Bible has a lot of names for the likes of her, and you can be sure she came to no good end."

"You said Mr. Simmons was watching Judy in case she turned out the same way as Wendy. What did he do to keep Judy from straying?"

"He read her scriptures, and told her over and over about what happened to her sister, so she could strengthen her will against immorality. But Judy was deceitful." I suspected that these were not her own words she was mouthing. "She pretended to be chaste while she was under our roof, so we wouldn't call her to task. But as soon as her foot was outside our door, she ran to Satan." She gave me a hard stare. "Beware the way of the debauched, young woman. You know the right words to say, but I can see you aren't among the saved. The time of reckoning is coming soon!" She closed the door with a bang.

I had almost reached the car when she opened the door and beckoned me back. Her voice pitched so low that I could hardly make out the words, she said, "If you find Judy, could you tell her to get in touch with Miss Trawick? That's her favorite teacher from high school. Miss Trawick could let me know Judy's all right."

"Miss Trawick—Yes, I promise I'll tell her. Thank you for your time."

"Don't come back here. If my husband knew I'd talked to you, he'd be terribly angry." She shut the door again.

CHAPTER TWENTY-FOUR

I sat in the car, parked next to an unkempt public park, listening to country music on the radio and Pugsley's grunting complaints, drinking weak takeout coffee and chewing on a stale cinnamon roll. It all fit my state of mind. Too bad I didn't have a pickup and a devoted hound instead of an iffy Toyota and a pug with attitude. The pendulum was swinging back again, and my sympathies for Kelly/Judy were restored, after hearing about what her childhood must have been like. The Simmons family was definitely case study material. One daughter dead, one missing to the greater glory of Mr. Simmons' vengeful Old-Testament God.

Then there was her journal. I kept returning to the last days recorded in the notebook, not knowing what I was looking for.

Sept. 9. Today when I was dusting her little glass animals I dropped one. It broke into a million pieces. I swept up all the bits and put them in a garbage can on the street. God, please don't let her notice that it's gone. I don't know what she'd do if she knew I broke it. She says she can tell if I lie about anything.

Sept. 13. I keep having dreams where I get better and I tell her I'm leaving. When I wake up, I'm afraid she'll guess what was in the dream, and cancel my next session, or hit me.

Sept. 15. She never touches me anymore. Now I wish she would, at least I'd feel like I was real. I don't think she notices me except to tell me about what I didn't get clean enough. I'm going to talk to her about it Monday.

This was the last entry, written days before "Kelly" went missing. The first time I read it, I speculated that this small burst of spirit might have brought retribution from Moira. This time when I put it down, I considered other possible reasons for this being the last entry.

I decided to call Judy's high school English teacher, Miss Trawick, before returning to San Francisco. Her name conjured up a genteel spinster lady given to wearing print dresses and enamored of Wordsworth. I hoped she was retired. It was more likely that she'd be at home midday. Luck was with me. First, a Phyllis Trawick was listed in the local directory. Second, although she sounded decades away from retirement, she was at home with a sprained ankle. She agreed to see me right away.

In front of her house, I gave Pugsley a stern warning not to bark, slobber on the windows or chew up the Kleenex box, and slid out of the door. This was his cue for evasive action. He dodged and faked a nip on my arm when I swept him back inside. Fifteen minutes earlier we had taken an indulgent romp through a park, where he had sniffed and lifted his leg as often as he liked. He did not appear to remember this.

Before I could ring the buzzer, the door was held open wide for me by a wiry man in his mid-twenties, wearing a Nine Inch Nails T-shirt and cotton drawstring pants. This must be Sean, whom Phyllis Trawick had called "my man." In San Francisco the sight of a straight man with a head of cropped blond fuzz, a crystal dangling from one ear, and a small nose-ring would not draw a second glance. Here in the hinterlands, he was wildly exotic. He gave me a dazzling smile and introduced himself.

147

Sean laughed at the sight of Pugsley's frog-face pressed against the car window and insisted that the dog was welcome too. The wretched cur barked smugly as I fetched him from the car.

Sean showed me into a sunny bedroom filled with plants and books. Ensconced on a patchwork quilt with a pair of purring cats was a large cocoa-skinned woman. From what I knew about her she was probably in her early forties, though she looked closer to my age. Her bandaged foot and ankle were propped on a stack of pillows. Pugsley trotted toward the bed, preparing to spring up and join them. I stopped him with a tug on his leash. He sat on my feet, emitting a snort of frustration.

"Hi, Maggie, come on in. You're a godsend. I'm so bored I told my next-door neighbor she could braid my hair this afternoon, and I never sit still that long! How about a cup of coffee? It's the good stuff from Peet's." I shook her hand and happily agreed to a cup. "Sean, sweetheart, would you?"

Sean gave Phyllis a knowing grin and turned to Pugsley. "Come on fella, let's do male bonding in the kitchen while the women talk." With unheard-of obedience, Pugsley jauntily followed Sean. I sank into a puffy boudoir chair beside the bed.

Phyllis lowered her voice. "I had to get him out of here. They always talk about women being gossips, but my honey cannot keep a secret to save his soul. How can I help you?"

"Tell me about Judy. Anything, whether you think it's important or not."

"I taught English to both Judy and her sister Wendy. I didn't get to know Judy very well. Wendy was the one who sought me out for confidences."

"All I know about her is that she was a lesbian, and she committed suicide."

"Wendy would volunteer to help after class. I could tell she was trying to get up the courage to talk to me. Finally she let down her guard, and what she told me about her father made

148

the hairs on the back of my neck stand on end. He beat her and Judy, who was still in grade school, for the sake of their souls. He told them they were worthless, empty vessels. To this day, I can still hear her saying that. I suggested getting a social worker out to their house, which frightened her so much that she refused to talk to me anymore. So after that, all I had were observations. For example, Wendy brought different clothes to school with her to change into—nothing particularly daring, but Papa wouldn't allow his daughters to wear slacks, let alone jeans. Their skirts were always ankle length, and of course makeup was out of the question. When Judy turned thirteen, she repeated the same pattern."

"I knew kids who did that kind of thing when I was in school, but it didn't seem to scar them."

"You're right, if it had only been a matter of clothes, well, inventive teenagers get around that. I believe Mr. Simmons used the Bible and God as an excuse for hating women, and especially any sign of independence in women. Those girls were fighting for their self-worth."

"Do you remember when it was that Judy came to you?"

"It was around the fifth anniversary of Wendy's death. Judy was only ten when it happened. She knew I had taught Wendy, and she desperately needed someone to talk to about Wendy's suicide. Wendy and another girl had run off together. They were hitch-hiking, trying to get to Los Angeles. Somehow, Mr. Simmons tracked them down. He dragged Wendy back home and locked her up in her room. Three months later, Wendy committed suicide."

"What a sad story," I said, "and what a terrible thing for Judy to grow up knowing about her sister. Did you know Wendy's friend, the one she tried to run away with?"

"No, she wasn't from around here. Judy didn't know the girl's name, I remember, but she was determined to find it out. Anyway, when Judy came to see me, I tried to persuade her to get counseling. I also told her about my sister Eleanor. Eleanor came out as a lesbian when she was sixteen, and there was open warfare in my family until she went to live with our great-auntie in Missouri. She made it through, and now she's a college dean. My daddy even let her come to our parents' golden wedding anniversary party—without her partner. Of course, I wasn't allowed to bring my white boy lover, either." She sighed, and stroked a very pregnant tabby that was curled at her knees.

"Anyway, I'd begun to get a sense of how much Judy blamed Wendy's death on her relationship with that other girl—though the only thing she knew was that the two girls were in bed together when Mr. Simmons found them. I tried to counter what Judy was getting from her loving family about the wrath of Jehovah. Considering her father's attitudes about women, you can guess what he'd think about lesbians."

"Yes, I can. I experienced quite a dose of hell and damnation when I came out in Iowa. How did Judy react?"

"Not well," Phyllis said. "She was furious with me. She wanted to confide in me, but she didn't want me to meddle, and she certainly didn't want me to tell her that Wendy's lover, the woman she'd picked out to play Satan, had been a seventeen-year-old girl in love. She charged out of the room, and that was the last time we talked until a few weeks ago, when she called me."

"Can you tell me about it?"

"She called in the middle of the night, so my memory is a little muddled. She asked me how my sister realized she was gay. It sounded urgent, so I didn't complain about her waking me up. I told her what Eleanor told me. It was when she was twelve years old and she enjoyed wrestling with her friend Amy far more than Amy did, or than any girl was supposed to. I tried to ask Judy how she was and where she was, and she hung up. I haven't heard from her since."

"Was she asking about herself?"

"My guess is yes, but it's hard to think of Judy as a sexual being, period. That was one sick family she came from. She was very bright, very intense, the kind you expect to write dark poetry. She had her own set of absolute values in opposition to the ones her parents tried to instill."

"Have you heard any news about her over the years?"

"Just that she'd finally left home a few years ago. She didn't go to college, got a job in a restaurant nearby and stayed at home with her parents. She didn't have any friends left around here, so word about her wouldn't get around."

Sean brought in a tray of coffee and homemade walnut cookies, and we all socialized for a few minutes. Sean told me how he'd fallen in love with Phyllis when he was a junior in Phyllis' home room. He kept his passion a secret until two years after he graduated, then turned up on Phyllis' doorstep with a dozen roses and his declaration of love.

"It took me two more years to wear her down," he said proudly.

"Work, work, work!" chuckled Phyllis.

They planned to be married the following spring. I offered them congratulations, feeling craven for my envy of their easy affection.

The two exchanged a significant glance, and Sean withdrew with his cup. Phyllis shifted her position on the bed so she could face me head-on.

"This hasn't been much help, has it?" she asked.

"I don't know yet. Were there any friends she might have stayed in contact with, anyone her mother wouldn't know about?"

"She had a couple of friends. One of them, Michael Welton, went off to New York. I heard he was involved in theater set design there. He was about as openly gay as you can be here in the sticks. He died of AIDS last year." She saw my surprise. "I know, it's a contradiction, that's the marvelous thing about human beings, isn't it? I always figured her other friend would come out some day, too. Her name is Beth Homan. She was a grad student in Berkeley, but I haven't heard anything about her for a few years."

I thanked Phyllis for her insights and Sean for his hospitality. Pugsley didn't want to leave, and I had to drag him to the car. Traffic on the way back to San Francisco was at a crawl, but it gave me lots of time to try to integrate the Simmons' desolate child into the adult woman who had acted so many roles before disappearing.

CHAPTER TWENTY-FIVE

We finally came into view of the San Francisco skyline, and I felt that familiar pang of returning to my turf that even the shortest trip out of the city evokes in me. Sure, it's got a serious earthquake habit, a bozo board of supervisors, too much crime, no decent art in the museums. But as the Angel said in Tony Kushner's *Perestroika,* heaven is a city much like San Francisco. I have come mighty close to kissing the ground on returning from, say, Nonesuch, Iowa.

During the entire excursion I hadn't seen any surveillance. It was always possible that I had missed a tailing vehicle, but I was pretty good. Jack had taught me the art of avoiding surveillance as well as conducting it. Perhaps Parker Security didn't send its agents outside city limits.

I went right to the office. When we passed the Cable Car Turnaround a few steps from my building, Pugsley drew considerable attention from the bored tourists waiting in line. A Swiss couple insisted on taking his picture. He preened and pranced, and again I had to tug him with me brutishly. One of the men hanging out in the lobby of my building looked familiar. Presumably one of my spooks.

I called the city's Missing Persons Unit, as I had threatened Scott Bentley I would do, though I left out the part about him. Voicemail picked up. So much for unfolding drama, or thanks for helping the police with their inquiries. I left a message for the investigator in charge of Kelly/Judy's case, giving him Judy's full name and the address of her parents. It was only right to share these facts, now that I'd gotten all I could out of the Simmonses.

I faxed Howard Ericson an updated report on my visits with Mrs. Simmons and Phyllis Trawick, and my intention of following up with Beth Homan. Then I faxed the official one to Robert Summers. The phone number Sylvia had given me was a voicemail box, and in my message I summarized what I had told Howard and Summers.

I had managed to inform all three without personal contact, for which I was sincerely grateful. That distasteful task completed, I tried all the easy-schmeazy skip tracing techniques on Beth Homan. None of them got me an address or phone number. If she was still in the Bay Area, it would take some digging to find her. I called Ricardo at home.

"Ready to find me another one?"

"Sure! Except I can't do it tonight. Ludo got tickets to Pearl Jam. But I can go in first thing tomorrow morning."

"That's soon enough. All we have on her is her name, Beth Homan, and that she was a grad student at Berkeley. I tried all the basics, and she's not listed in directories or with utilities, and doesn't have a driver's license. I have to turn it over to you, maestro."

"Piece of cake. A name is more than you gave me on that guy last month." He was really enjoying this and I stifled a sisterly desire to take him down a peg. "You know, Maggie, you ought to get out tonight, too. Take a break from this stuff!"

"Since you mention it, I do have a date tonight. I'll see you tomorrow. Have a good time, and don't forget to take along plenty of condoms."

"Aw, Maggie, you're worse than my mom . . . ."

There was another woman I wanted to find, but without even a name, birthplace or description, it was hopeless. All I knew was that Wendy's girlfriend would be in her early thirties. She could be living anywhere by now. She might even be dead, like Wendy.

One last call, to Chad at his home number. I left him a message about Kelly's real identity and asked him to pass it along as he saw fit. I wanted this girl to be found far more than I wanted the credit for finding her.

There wasn't anything else I could think of to do, and besides, my blind date at Jessie and Tate's house awaited. Oh joy.

I drove to my cottage, trying not to think about what coming home from work on a Friday night would feel like if I were a corporate legal assistant. Probably my week would not include breaking and entering or combing my hair compulsively to make sure I didn't have lice . . . .

I dished out food for the creatures. Pugsley made a play for the cats' food dish, and they boxed his nose, almost in tandem. They didn't give him as much slack as usual because he had been away all day, and they didn't recognize him as their couch mate. He gave a heartbreaking whine and snuffled away at his own food.

I shut myself in the bedroom away from the drama outside. After standing in front of my closet for a full five minutes, willing the perfect outfit to call attention to itself, I gave up and grabbed a skinny pair of pants and snug top. At least the woman would see what she might be getting.

I was fishing around under the dresser for an earring, cursing the cats' propensity to bat them around until they fell on the floor, where they got vacuumed up, when the phone rang. "It's not Diana, you dolt, not on a Friday night," I told myself sternly, lunging for it before it had a chance to ring a second time.

It was Leslie from Nature's Harmony Foods. "Maggie, things

have gone crazy—Jerry has split town. GT says it's because Jerry's ex-wife has got a court order on him for child support, but Cecelia heard that he was about to be indicted for trying to bribe one of the health inspectors. Anyway, before he split, he called everybody into his office, one by one, to ask us about you!"

"Interesting. What did he want to know?"

"What you were really doing at the store. He said he went by the address you gave him to bring you a present—we can guess what the present was—and of course you weren't there. So he called S.F. State, and found out you're not a student, not to mention that there's no Alternative Retail program. He was so scared, I almost felt sorry for him. Do you think he might have done something to Kelly?"

"I guess it's possible, but I think it's more likely he's afraid I'm an undercover state inspector, or even a private eye working for his ex-wife. Thanks for calling, I know it bothered you to call the other ISA members."

"Oh, that's all right. I talked to my sponsor and she said I should turn it over."

"Didn't anybody at the store tell Jerry what I was doing there?"

"No, everyone loved watching him squirm."

CHAPTER TWENTY-SIX

I rarely agree to Jessie's matchmaking attempts, and when I do I always regret it. Tate stays clear of Jessie's meddling, *and* she believes in truth in advertising, so my plan was to get there early, grab Tate, and interrogate her about my sculptor/neighbor date. If this woman had left Los Angeles because all the lesbians in that town had been burned by her, Tate would tell me. Jessie would call that being negative.

"Hello, Maggie, I'm Brenda." Brenda Milton had beat me to it. She was alone on the deck, stretched out on the redwood lounger I often snagged for myself, so my first impression of her was long tanned legs in bike shorts. Sweeping back masses of black hair, she slowly unfolded from the lounger and approached me with an assured stride. She had to be 6' 2". It was a novel sensation to look up at anyone, particularly another woman. She was wearing a tunic made from hand-dyed Indonesian fabric over the shorts, and stacks of gold bracelets clacked with her every movement.

"I'm glad to finally meet you . . . Jessie's told me so much about you." She was overtly sizing me up. Suddenly shy and trying not to think about what exactly Jessie might have said, I made nice.

Tate stepped out of the house carrying a tray of iced tea, a quizzical expression on her face.

"I see you've met, with no help from anyone." She turned toward the house and yelled, "Jessie Louise, your dinner guests are here. Get off that phone!" To us: "She's organizing a breast cancer lobbying day in Sacramento—next month. Somehow this translates into emergency phone calls tonight."

Jessie rolled out of the house wearing the lime green suit and purple blouse she must have worn to work that day. "I always forget how time-consuming it can be to get women to do the same thing at the same time. Everybody wants input!" she complained, rubbing her right ear. She took the tray out of Tate's hands and gave it to me. Then she gave Tate a lingering kiss. How much of this was in adoration of Tate and how much was to set a tone for Brenda and me? Jessie plays a deep game. It was an impressive kiss, I grant them that.

Brenda shot me an inquiring glance. I grinned. Jessie was in true form tonight.

While Tate examined the fish that had been roasting in foil on the grill, Jessie and I set the table on the deck. Jessie was telling Brenda about her activist group, Cancer Rising, and I half-listened, enjoying the sounds of women's voices. It was a relief to be away from the investigation, though I did look forward to talking to Jessie and Tate about it later.

Brenda watched Jessie toss the salad and told us all about the difficulties she was having with her work. The couple in the house next door to her had a new baby, and it cried all the time, especially at night. She had spoken sharply to the couple, but they refused to take control over the situation. And there was a rooster in the neighborhood, obviously breaking zoning laws, which woke her up every day. I caught Tate making a face at Jessie when she thought no one else was looking. Jessie shot both of us a keep-an-open-mind look.

I went into entertainer mode and told some stories about the bizarre things people thought they could hire a P.I. to do. Jessie piped in with a few lawyers-not-recognizable-as-humans stories. As secretary to a senior partner in a major firm, Jessie has an endless supply of these. Most are true. Brenda ate steadily.

Tate asked if Brenda was enjoying her studio, which had been the pride of the artist who built it. Brenda responded that the workmen painting her kitchen insisted on talking to each other, or worse, playing the radio, which destroyed her concentration. Jessie made sympathetic noises, but I intercepted the grimace she showed Tate.

Tate told us about the trials of doing hypnotherapy in the midst of earthquake retrofitting of her office building, including the creative incorporation of jackhammer sounds into the client's healing process. Jessie and I were laughing so hard that we were pounding the table by the time she finished. Brenda turned the conversation to art, and shared with us her disillusionment with the art community in San Francisco compared to the one in L.A.

"Do you think it's possible you haven't had time to make the kind of contacts here that you had in L.A.?" suggested Tate.

"I've met everyone who could be considered important here, certainly everyone with any claim of doing important work," Brenda said.

"You should see her work, Maggie," Tate interjected. "I've never seen anything like it."

"That's because no one is doing anything like it," replied Brenda.

"What medium do you work in?" I asked.

"Would it mean anything to you if I told you, or are you just trying to make conversation?"

"I might be able to tell the difference between, say, stone and Play-Doh," I said, through my teeth.

"I've offended you. I'm sorry," she said, not sounding particularly sorry. "It's difficult finding people I can resonate with. I find that artists are a unique breed, and we need to be with our own kind. Could you pass the salmon?"

"I'm sorry," Jessie said, grinning ear to ear, "we're saving that for Maggie's cats. They're also a unique breed, and it's so hard to find salmon they can resonate with. Thank you so much for coming." She gestured toward the steps leading from the deck down to the back alley.

Brenda didn't grasp that she was being eighty-sixed.

Tate stood too and extended her hand to Brenda. When Brenda took it she found herself being gently tugged toward the stairs. "Do let us know when you have your show. We'll all stand about and scratch our heads over what you're trying to convey."

"Well!" said Brenda, her clogs clattering down the wooden stairs.

"Well!" the three of us remaining said.

"Jessie, don't you screen these women at all before you throw them at Maggie?" scolded Tate, chasing the last cherry tomato around the inside of the salad bowl with her fork.

"No, she does not!" I said, buttering the last piece of cornbread. "I just happened to have a witness tonight."

"You know I only want you to be as happy as Tate and I are, darling," Jessie said, abashed. "Besides, now you know someone doing important work!"

I threw the unbuttered half of my cornbread at her. Jessie cleared the table and Tate made coffee. I stretched out on the lounge chair, half-listening to Jessie and Tate debate marinade ingredients. Their comfortable domesticity made me wistful about Diana, and tonight's disastrous matchmaking had confirmed my worst fears that I was going to live the rest of my life single.

I waited what I thought was a discreet amount of time before bringing up Moira, Judy, Sylvia, Howard, et al. They burst into laughter, and immediately checked their watches.

"What is so funny?" I glared at them until Jessie took pity on me and explained.

"I bet Tate you'd hold out for at least ten minutes after Brenda left. She said you wouldn't be able to wait and would lure me away for a one-on-one while Brenda was here. Pay up, sucker-bait!" she crowed to Tate.

"Jessie! And I can't believe *you'd* bet on it, Tate!"

"I'm sorry we made fun of you, Maggie, we really do want to help with this," Tate said, with a small final hiccup of laughter.

I told them everything that had happened so far. Jessie is my regular confidante on cases. She's an attentive listener, and in describing the principals in a case, I frequently remember important details in the telling. Tate usually leaves us to it, but she had a personal stake in this case.

The tangled story of Judy/Kelly took a long time to tell. I turned to Tate: "Why do you think she went to all those 12-step groups?"

"Could be as simple as loneliness. She grew up isolated, and it didn't get any better for her. If she couldn't confide about what was actually wrong, talking about made-up addictions would at least get people's sympathetic attention."

"And if you wanted to pretend you were an alcoholic, or a codependent person, or an incest survivor, it would be a good place to get tips on how to act," Jessie said.

I told them about my middle-of-the-night encounter with the bottle-and-can man. This horrified them so greatly that I couldn't get them to discuss what he had told me about a "big, rich woman." I changed the subject. Howard's consternation that I wasn't butch enough made an entertaining story.

"I think there's a business opportunity in there somewhere," Tate said, her eyes narrowed. "Don't look the part for your job? We'll make you over so you fit everyone's favorite stereotype! Maggie, your outfit is all wrong, you have to give up light beer and switch to bourbon. And practice a sultry expression. You should look as if you might be dangerous."

"But even more important than that," Jessie piped in, "you'll have to start smoking again—Camel straights!"

"Perfect for the Ericsons! Maggie works for such delightful people," Tate said.

"Thanks to you!" Jessie shot an accusing glance at Tate. "Maggie should go back to working exclusively for gay clients."

"As if there weren't sleazy rich lesbians and gays—" Tate interrupted.

"Moira *is* gay, that's how I got into this, remember?" I protested. "Besides, I've met interesting people on this case." I told them about Leslie at Nature's Harmony, Patrick at the Symphony and Lisa the baby hooker. Romantic-to-the-core Jessie loved the story of Phyllis Trawick's courtship by her determined young lover.

"But you still haven't found the girl."

"No, we have more scattered bits of information about her, but they don't connect. She's still a mystery and I'm still at a loss about how to find her."

"All things considered, everyone might be better off if she remained unfound," Jessie said thoughtfully.

"If I knew she was alive somewhere, I think I could embrace failure on this one," I answered.

CHAPTER TWENTY-SEVEN

The alarm was right next to my head, and its shrill ring made me levitate a couple of inches as I tried to remember where I was. It was even worse after I remembered. Bits of sandy matter had settled on my eyelashes. I longed for my cottage, for a hot shower in a place where I wouldn't have to prop a chair under the doorknob of the communal bathroom to keep my neighbors out. I settled for washing at the grimy sink and sticking my head under the tap for a few seconds. The cold water was good for waking me up and flushing the sediment out of my eyes. I consoled myself with the thought that my lank hair and unpressed clothes made me fit in better with my neighbors.

I made coffee with my electric hot pot and filter cone and tossed in some hot chocolate mix in place of milk. Breakfast was a rice cake spread with peanut butter. I had assured Liam that it would be like camping. It wasn't.

At eight-thirty I started my room-to-room visits. My ruse was a shoebox-size package, postmarked and well-wrapped, addressed to Kelly. At the first door, only a man's eyes and nose were visible through the chain-locked door. I told him the mail carrier had left this box with me, and as a new tenant, I didn't know anyone. Did he know Kelly Henry? He looked at me as if I were crazy and slammed the door.

At the second door, an emaciated man with multiple tracks

on his arms reached for the package, saying "Yeah, I'm Kelly." I didn't let go, and stared him down.

"Okay, okay," he said. "What's goin' on?"

"I'm trying to find a friend who lived on the third floor until last month. It's hard to get anybody to open their door these days. This is just a way to start conversations." I flashed Kelly's photo at him. He gave it a perfunctory glance.

"She the kiddy prostitute? You ought to see some of the zombies she takes upstairs!" This man's skin was bluish gray. If anyone could declare his expertise on the living dead, it was him.

"You're thinking of Lisa."

"Sorry, I lost interest in sex awhile ago, and now you all pretty much look alike to me." He shut the door.

There was no response to my knocks at the next few doors, although I could hear movement inside a couple of rooms. Then I hit two doors of families, Laotian or Cambodian, I guessed, with whom communication was limited to head shakes and smiles. On my next try, a quavery voice asked who was there. I gave my story and the door edged open. A Latino boy, who couldn't be over 17, but looked like people I'd seen in the final stages of AIDS wasting, leaned in the doorway.

"My name's Maggie. I'm trying to find Kelly Henry." I held up the photo. "Do you know her?"

"I think so. I can't remember a lot of things I used to know. Does she live here?"

"She did. She's missing now."

He took the photo and studied it for a few seconds. "Okay, yeah, I did see her a few times."

"Do you remember her having visitors?"

"One night I seen this Kelly going up the stairs with an old *anglo* lady. I figured it was her mother, coming to give her shit about being here. They were real mad at each other, that's why I remember. Around here, if somebody looks mad, you move out of the way, 'cause you might get shot by accident when they go off."

"Do you remember what the woman looked like?"

"Nice clothes. She was about fifty, blonde, good shape for her age, I guess."

"Anything else?"

"No, like I told you, I don't remember stuff like I used to."

I left him with a twenty and my business card.

No one answered at the next two doors, and the third was opened by an ancient Chinese woman who put a handkerchief over her mouth and cowered away as if I were a plague-bearer. I talked myself into giving it one last try.

The door was opened an inch. A bent-over woman with abundant white braids, without doubt the "Mexican witch" Al had described, squinted up at me from behind two chain locks. With majestic deliberation she unlatched them. "Hello. You Jehovah Witness?" This was said with such anticipation that I assumed she was one of their faithful.

"No, I'm not. Hello, I'm Maggie Garrett."

"Ah." She mastered her disappointment and smiled broadly. "Well, I am Señora Morales. Come in, come into my house."

She opened the door wide. Smells that took me back to my great-great aunts' attic wafted past her: mostly mothballs, but also a floral scent and something else—vanilla? She led me into a dark room crowded with old furniture. She turned on an overhead light, and I faced the stares of generations of ancestors, posed stiffly in lacquered wood frames on every vertical or horizontal surface. Many had the same beaky nose as my hostess. Señora Morales urged me to sit on the ancient formal sofa. I sat, and a cloud of dust flew up and hung in the air around me. A long-haired black cat woke at this, and shot me a hostile glance from its nest in a pillowy chair trimmed with yards of fringe.

"Señora Morales, I'm staying upstairs and I'm trying to find

165

out about a young *anglo* woman named Kelly who lived here."
Again I produced Kelly's photo. "Do you know her?"

"I don't know her, but I see her many times." She shook her
head sadly. "Very unhappy girl. You want a fruit drink?"

"No, but thank you. Why do you say she was unhappy?"

"I have the gift, what you call 'second sight.' That's why I
asked are you Jehovah people. They come around all the time. I
make them crazy!" I could see that she was cranking up to tell
Watchtower torture stories, and moved to cut her off.

"What did your sight tell you about Kelly?"

She squinted at my face closely before answering. "You believe me, you believe I can see things? Good girl! This Kelly had
many lost souls in her body, all fighting. Perhaps she is at peace
now."

"You think she is dead?"

"*Sí.* And you . . . my sight tells me you are not at ease. Someone wants to harm you, *verdad?*"

I thought about the men tailing me. "Could be. I'll watch my
back. Can you tell me anything else about Kelly?"

"Her visitors—*muy extraños,* very strange. Now that other
girl, the little *puta,* her visitors I can understand. The men pay
her, take her like a dog, and go away. But one young man came
to see this Kelly, and there was a rich woman I saw here two
times. Both of them so angry when they come. Why would
people like that come here, I asked myself. How about chocolate, I make you hot chocolate?"

"No, thanks, I'm fine. Can you describe these people?"

"The man looked like a homosexual, but *muy macho,* not like
those men on the television who wear dresses." I pulled out the
photo of Scott that Sylvia had given me. Señora Morales put her
face close to the picture, then held it at arm's length. "*Sí,* this is
the one."

"Do you remember when he was here?"

"It was the anniversary of my husband's death, September 4."

"Did you hear them talk?"

"No, they go to her room, he comes down in five minutes, like I told you, very angry."

"And the woman?"

"Yellow hair, not like the baby *prostituta*, but so light! Her clothes like in a magazine. When I saw her face I was surprised. She was no longer a young woman."

"Do you remember when she was here?"

She rubbed her chin with a floury hand, saw what she had done and chuckled at herself. "First time, maybe two months ago. Last time, two-three weeks."

"Did you see them together?"

"*Sí,* the first time. They came in the door together, but not talking."

"And the second time? That was two or three weeks ago?"

"*Sí.* It was late at night. I heard a noise, and I looked out my door to see is it my no-good grandson drunk and falling down the steps again. But it is this woman. She comes down the stairs so fast, looking all around. She sees me and *she* almost falls down the steps. She is afraid to be in this building." She gave a short bark of a laugh. "That one is right to be afraid of us here in this place. We could live for a long time on the ring she had on one finger."

"Can you be more exact about the day of the week you saw this woman?"

"No, I'm sorry. Since I don't go to work anymore, I don't mark the days that way."

"Do you go to church?"

"Ah, *sí.*"

"Maybe that would help you remember if it was a Sunday?"

"*Mi niña,* I go to mass every day!"

I thanked her and turned down her offer of Nescafé. As if it were a daily occurrence, she accepted fifty bucks and my business card, and promised to call me if she remembered anything else.

I stopped by Lisa's room to show her Scott's photo, but her padlock was still on, as it had been when I passed it earlier. She must have been out all night. I shivered at the thought of a fourteen year old with no friends or resources on the street at night.

It was past the time I had planned to be at the office. The Titan Trust decision-makers were meeting in special session this afternoon, and my contract bid was on their agenda. They wanted all the investigators on their short list to be available for phoned-in questions.

On the drive in, I thought about Señora Morales' bombshell. I was sure that the aging blonde she described was Sylvia Ericson. That meant Sylvia had been seen at Kelly's house not only at the time she'd told me about, but on an earlier date as well. Why give me that line about honesty and openness and only tell me part of the story? I wondered if Señora Morales saw Scott the same night that Lisa saw him go into Kelly's room with her. Or had he been to the house more than once, too? I'd have to press Lisa about when exactly she saw him.

My morning's work had not gone the way I'd planned. Things were getting murkier by the minute.

CHAPTER TWENTY-EIGHT

Ricardo looked up from the phone with a ferocious scowl when I opened the office door. The warning wasn't necessary. I knew better than to laugh at the convincing falsetto he was using to get access to grad student records on a Saturday when school offices were closed. He thrust several message slips into my hand, not losing a beat in the story he was weaving: parents gravely injured, their only daughter had to be found immediately. I poured a cup of coffee and shut myself in my office to give him privacy.

The "urgent" box was checked on each of the message forms. Chad Osafune wanted me to call him immediately. Liam was at his job and needed to talk to me *soon*. The third message was a demand that I stay in the office to receive a call from Howard Ericson.

Before I could consider whom to try first, the phone rang and I picked it up. A woman from Titan Trust, who identified herself only as Tara, told me she needed to record my responses to a hypothetical situation involving a fraudulent claim for job-injury disability. The Titan Trust selection committee would then analyze my answers. I started listing procedures until I realized that I was not being recorded. Tara was taking verbatim notes, and she didn't know shorthand. We established how far behind I had left her, and I picked up the narrative.

Ricardo bounced in, waving a sheet of paper, and did the

Church Lady superiority dance around my desk. He handed me a phone number and address for Judy's friend Beth Homan. I smiled my congratulations. He stayed to listen to my laborious description of the fictitious investigation, and rolled his eyes when she had me spell "likelihood."

A call came in on the other line, and Ricardo lunged into his outer chamber to get it. He had to be waiting for a personal call. A few minutes later, he stuck his head in and mimed that he was leaving for the weekend, and that someone was on the other line for me. I blew him a kiss and asked Tara if she could hold. She sounded relieved. Even at our snail's pace I suspected she had fallen behind again and welcomed the chance to catch up.

It was Chad Osafune. He said Paolo was out sick, so he'd got stuck doing a surveillance job with another man from the Glass Agency, whom he summed up as a "racist lump of lard." Chad had offered to fetch coffee and donuts to get away from the lard lump and call me. He couldn't take much more of this, he complained. It was about time for another career switch . . . The longer he went on, the more uneasy I became. Chad never talked this much.

"Chad, what is it?"

"Um, I'm sorry, Maggie. Well . . . your girl Judy is dead. Some kids found her body at China Basin yesterday." A strangled sound came from somewhere in my throat. Pain, defeat, frustration, anger, all mixed in. The only emotional component missing was shock. Like Lisa, I had grown used to thinking of her in the past tense.

"What? You okay, Maggie?"

"No, but go on. How'd you find out about her?"

"Well, I put out the word to a few friends on the force. One of them—we go all the way back to the LAPD—called me this morning. He says they're treating it as murder."

"Why not suicide or accident?"

"Because the body was in one of those extra-heavy nylon bags with a zipper, you know the ones that look like a giant version of a gym bag? I see them in stores and I always think, 'you could put a body in there!' Well, somebody did. And whoever put her in the bag also stuck in a bunch of weights to keep her down. They're gonna be disappointed she didn't stay down there."

"You said the kids found her yesterday?"

"Yeah, but there was no ID on the body, so she was logged in as a Jane Doe. Then, based on the info you gave them, Missing Persons made the connection and called her folks. Can you believe it, her dad said he wasn't going to drive all the way to the city to identify her!"

Chad was going on about how a father might disown his daughter, but no mother ever could. Part of my brain took in what he said. Another part of me was somewhere far off, screaming. I'd been to that place before, when people I loved died of cancer or AIDS, when Ricardo's classmates got killed in drive-by shootings.

I interrupted Chad. "Was she dead when she went in?"

"No autopsy results yet. The guys working the case are real interested in Moira Ericson again."

"Who's got the case?"

"Joe Marcucci and his partner, um . . . it's some hyphenated combo, like Kinoshita-Costa."

Not Detective Diana Hoffman. I told myself that this was a good thing. Having to deal with her as a cop right now would be more than I could handle. I thanked Chad and hung up.

Judy was dead. She had torn through people's lives, blowing the covers off their secrets. She was no longer a problem to them, or her family—just to the police, and anyone who was suspected of her murder.

And to me, although I'd probably be out of a job now. Judy

had turned up with little help from me. That must be what Howard Ericson was in such a rush to talk about. Finally he was free to tell me what he really thought of me, since he'd have no more need of my services, unless the Ericsons wanted me to build up a defense for Moira. The police would be taking a hard look at the allegations in Judy's journal now.

Oh my God, Tara from Titan Trust was still holding on the other line! I gave myself a few seconds to make the transition and pushed the button to reconnect. For this round, she wanted me to enact a new scenario, even more loaded toward catching any unseemly sympathies for defrauders. This one involved a single mother of four who was claiming complete disability. I groaned, closed my eyes, and saw Jack Windsor winking at me. Then I answered with the truth instead of what I knew they wanted. This time Tara didn't ask for the repetition of any long words; nor did she bother to hide her disillusionment with me. Her scramble to get off the phone was so obvious that I burst into laughter as I hung up on her.

"Thanks, Jack," I said, "but if you want to help, how about next week's winning Lotto combination?" Before I could even heat up my coffee, Howard Ericson called.

"I've only got a couple of minutes. I'm on my way to New York. Have you heard about Moira?" He was shouting into an airport pay phone.

"No. Have you heard about Judy Simmons?"

"That's why I'm calling. The police found a ring on the girl's body that belonged to Moira. They decided that the ring and the journal were enough to bring her back for questioning!"

"Did they book her?"

"No, but she's scared to death. She thinks it's just a matter of time before they arrest her."

"How can I help?"

"Find out more background on this girl. It's almost as if she killed herself to frame Moira, but she couldn't have . . ."

"Mr. Ericson—"

"Maybe I should have told you more at the beginning, but I didn't think it made a difference. If only we could have persuaded Moira to get involved . . ." His voice trailed off, and he cleared his throat, pulling himself together.

"I'll do everything I can." In spite of myself, I was sympathizing with him. "Is there anything you could tell me now that might help Moira?"

"I've got to go. My flight's leaving. Our separate deal is still on. Anything private about me, you *keep* it private. I'll be back in San Francisco Sunday night."

"Mr. Ericson, it's different when murder is involved—"

"Send me two statements. I'll see you get paid." He hung up.

So much for sympathy. He was still an arrogant jerk determined to cover his own butt. Absently I poured out the last of the coffee, trying to assimilate the events of the past few minutes.

I dialed Sylvia's contact number and left a message asking whether she still wanted me to meet her at the Barbary Club for brunch the next day. I had no heart for it. Besides, she'd have no reason to talk to me privately now. My job for her had been to find Judy alive and give Sylvia the chance to speak with her ahead of Howard Ericson.

Liam wasn't at his desk when I called, so I left my itinerary on his voicemail. I had eliminated myself from Titan's selection process, so I saw no reason for sticking around the office.

I returned to the house on Capp Street to see Lisa, but her door was still padlocked from the outside. I left a note asking her to call me, with both of my numbers, under her door. Señora Morales was waiting on the landing, holding a tall votive candle with a garish picture of the Virgin of Guadalupe on it.

"Take this, *niña,* it will keep you safe from the evil one."

"What evil one, *Señora?*"

"You are a good daughter, I can tell. The Blessed Virgin protects the pure." My mother would dispute the part about being a good daughter, and no one had called me pure for a very long time, but I've never turned away prayer, blessings or jujus. I thanked her and kept going.

CHAPTER TWENTY-NINE

Home again. At least this case was giving me a strong appreciation for my cottage. After a shower and a change into clean clothes, I made myself a grilled cheese/tomato/zucchini sandwich and sat down on the couch. I'd stayed in motion since Chad's call about Judy, and there had been no time to take it in.

One time my band got hired for an unusual gig: the memorial service for a gay rocker who'd died of AIDS. None of the band members had known him, and we had a fairly callous attitude about it until we got there. During a part of the service called "Remembering Frank," friends and members of his family told touching or funny stories about him. He'd been a loving, generous man, and an audacious fighter for HIV services. After the eighth person got up and talked about how knowing Frank had changed his life, I lost count. I wished I had known him. As a matter of fact, by the end of the service I felt that I did know him, and I mourned him.

I thought about Frank's memorial as I tried to sort out how I felt about Judy. When Wendy Simmons killed herself, she left her younger sister behind to bear the brunt of her father's suspicions. Every day Mr. Simmons reminded Judy that Wendy was dead because of her lesbian lover. Judy remained at home long after her few friends left for college. Then she broke away and took on several personalities and a false name. She sought out a therapist and then told everyone she met that the woman was abusing her. She took advantage of the man who befriended her and secretly took pictures of him having sex with his married employer. She let everyone at Nature's Harmony Foods think she was involved with the repulsive manager, but of the two, she was the one in control. Patrick had said she was like quicksilver. No two people would have agreed on who exactly she was. And Lisa, her neighbor at the flophouse, was the only one I'd met who remembered Judy lovingly. That was the saddest part of all.

My sandwich was still on the plate, cold and uneaten. I took a bite of it and considered what to do next. The momentum in the investigation had come from my desire to find and help Judy. I was still on the case, but my enthusiasm was gone. Now it was a dreary mop-up operation, a way to pay the rent, like helping with a huge filing for a law firm when I was temping. You tried not to think about the content of the case, put in your hours, and collected your paycheck.

I gave Pugsley the rest of the grilled cheese and started on the loose ends.

The woman who answered at Beth Homan's number told me she'd see if Beth could take the call. After a couple of minutes, a different woman came on the line.

"Hi, do you mind telling me who's calling?"

"Maggie Garrett. I'm a private investigator calling about Beth's friend Judy Simmons."

"Oh, hi, this *is* Beth. I'm ducking a collection agency. What about Judy?"

"I'm sorry to tell you, Judy is—she's dead." There was a gasp on the other end.

"Dead! Poor Judy . . . How did she die?"

"She was murdered. Her body was just found yesterday."

"If she's dead, what help can I be?"

"I think the police suspect the wrong person. I wondered if

you had heard from her recently."

"Yeah, I did talk to her a few weeks ago, for the first time in, oh wow, a year? She used to disapprove of me, so she'd feel sinful after talking to me, and while she was living at home, they wouldn't let her have any contact with me."

"Why?"

"Because I'm a dyke, and an artist and, worst of all, I'm happy!"

"Got it."

"I don't think I can fill in any blanks for you. When she called last month, she wouldn't say what was going on with her. She had a bunch of questions about what lesbians do in bed, what turned me on, all kinds of stuff."

"What about when you were in high school? Did she talk to you about her sister Wendy killing herself?"

"That's all she talked about for a year or so. Her fascist father locked Wendy up and wouldn't let anyone see her except their minister, and *he* told Wendy she was going to burn in hell! But Judy blamed Wendy's poor girlfriend. Talk about identifying with your oppressor!"

"Did she know the girlfriend's name?"

"Not till last year. I think that's why she called me that time. She was super-excited because she'd just found it out. I couldn't believe she was still so obsessed."

"Do you remember the girl's name?"

"Moira Ericson. I remember because I never heard of a real person with that name before."

"Moira—Of course." It was right in front of me all along. Judy wanted to destroy Moira and her family to avenge her sister.

"You know Moira? What's she like? I've been hearing about her forever—"

The call waiting buzz was sounding. I thanked Beth and told her I'd let her know what I learned about Judy.

The other caller was Sylvia Ericson. She was subdued, her voice quavering. She told me that she still needed my services, regardless of what Howard might tell me. I heard myself agree to keep our appointment at her club the following day. I didn't tell her about Moira's connection to Judy, partly because I was still absorbing the news myself, partly because I believed Moira should get the news before her stepmother did.

I dialed Moira Ericson's home number. I almost didn't recognize her at first. All the patronizing assurance had gone out of her voice.

"Your father told me about the police questioning you," I said.

"It was worse than the last time, worse than I could have imagined. I couldn't tell if they really suspect me or if that sort of thing is just routine to them."

"Did you have an attorney with you?"

"No, they weren't charging me, and they made it sound like things would escalate if I asked to bring an attorney into it."

"There's a new angle to the case that may help. Judy was Wendy Simmons' sister."

I heard a sharp intake of breath, then muffled sobbing.

"Moira, are you all right?"

"It's . . . it's just a shock, after all these years. My God, how stupid of me not to realize! Wendy's sister . . . There was even a family resemblance. How could I have missed it?"

"Do you feel able to talk about Judy now? It could be important."

"Yes, go ahead."

"People who knew Judy told me that she always held you responsible for Wendy's suicide. Did you know that?"

"No, I never met any of Wendy's family except her father. Wendy used to talk about them, of course, especially her father. Judy thought Wendy's death was my fault? I can't understand why. That horrible man shut Wendy away from her friends. He didn't even let her mother talk to her. I had nothing to do with it. Why would Kelly—Judy—blame me?"

"Because the same father who locked Wendy away was the one who interpreted Wendy's death to Judy. Her perceptions of what happened would be completely warped. I believe she was planning to set you up, that she only went to you for therapy to get material for her journal."

"I can't accept that . . . ."

"Everywhere she went, she told people that you were having sex with her, and that she was practically a slave in your house."

"That would make everything we did in therapy a lie. How could she come in every day and pretend to bare her soul, when all along . . . ."

"I don't know. I suspect some of what went on in your sessions *was* real. But to get back to the situation with the police, I don't think you told me everything before, and whatever your reasoning was then, I think it's time to tell everything—to me and the police."

"What do you mean?"

"Judy's journal gives a detailed description of your house, down to what day the garbage truck comes. She couldn't know that much from one short visit."

Moira was quiet again, but she wasn't crying this time. Knowing how therapists use silence, I waited it out. Finally, with some of the authority back in her voice, she said, "Anything I tell you is confidential, right?"

"That's right."

"I was afraid to tell you, or anyone for that matter, because it looks so bad. There are so many petty rules . . . you break at least one a day just to serve your clients. I let Judy pay off her final sessions by doing housecleaning for me. We had already terminated, and she didn't have any money. That kind of thing just isn't done, but I thought no one would ever need to find out. She told me it was a matter of honor for her to pay me, and she begged me to let her work it off." Moira paused, then said bitterly, "A matter of honor. She was telling me that she was going to destroy my life as a matter of honor and I didn't listen."

"Is that how she got your ring?"

"I noticed the ring was missing about a month ago. My mother left it to me, so it has sentimental value, but I almost never wear it. It could have been missing longer. Judy must have had something engraved on it. The police acted as if it's important, but they wouldn't tell me what it says."

"Did you tell them about Judy working in your home for you?"

"No, nothing."

"Moira, you're seriously underestimating the police. When they start tracing down your stories, you're going to look guilty."

"Nothing I could truthfully say at this point would help. She was my client. I did continue to see her against the policy of the Women's Therapy Center. I did let her work in my house to pay off her therapy."

"She really had you psyched out, didn't she?"

"What do you mean?"

"She figured out that you like to make up your own rules. That's how she got you to see her outside the Therapy Center, and to let her pay off her debt with housework. She couldn't have pulled off her plans if you had played by the book. Did she really make that emergency visit to your house? The one where you said you called a doctor for a prescription?"

"No. They'll try to get Dr. Singh to testify that I never called him about her, won't they?"

"Maybe not, because of confidentiality. Still, it's a shaky story. I strongly suggest that you not use it anymore."

"You wouldn't understand what it's like for someone like me, whose whole life is about getting at the truth. I'm not good at lying. But I had to account for her knowing about my house."

"And you knew what she said about you, and your house, because you read her journal, didn't you?"

"It was completely unprofessional to do it. It's the one thing I feel truly guilty about. I knew she had written about me, the police made that clear when they questioned me the first time. I told myself that it was my responsibility to learn her state of mind by reading the journal, so that if I saw Kelly—Judy—again in treatment, I'd be able to understand her better. But the truth is, I wanted to see what she said about me."

"What did you think, when you saw what she had written?"

"I assumed she had written it as a resistance to therapy. It never occurred to me that she had intended for anyone to see it. And now . . . I don't know what to do."

"I think it's time you got a lawyer of your own. Not somebody your father hires, but someone you trust to take your side."

"I suppose you're right."

"Moira, do you remember seeing anyone the day you went looking for Judy at her house?"

"I talked to that crazy man who pretends to manage the building, Al. I must have seen some other people, but I was so frightened of being in that place that I can't remember individuals."

"If you had seen a man with red dreadlocks and reddish brown skin, do you think you'd remember him?"

"I'm sure I would remember someone like that. No, I didn't see him. Why, do you suspect him of killing Judy?"

"No, it was just one more detail to check. If you think of anything that might help, let me know."

She hung up. Almost nothing she had told me in our first interview had been true. Was she telling the truth now?

No answer at Liam's place. I left new messages, fed the animals, and returned to the house on Capp Street.

I owed it to Lisa to tell her about Judy. There was nothing I could do for Judy now, but I could make sure Lisa was told about her death in a way that respected their friendship. Although the police must have returned to the house after Judy's body was found, Lisa would have made herself scarce. It wasn't in Al's interest to tell the cops about his under-age sex partner, either. I didn't want Lisa to find out about Judy from Al or one of the other tenants.

From the stairway I could see the note I'd stuck under Lisa's door earlier. I left a new one, asking her to come next door to see me. I looked (and sniffed) for the scavenger, but he wasn't in the hall, and I doubted that he had a paid-up room in the house.

Tonight I had brought a portable tape player, and R.E.M. kept me company until I dozed off.

CHAPTER THIRTY

Once asleep I stayed that way. I woke with a start to the sirens of a fleet of fire trucks tearing by. Full-strength morning sunlight made it through even the dirty window of my room. According to my watch, it was after ten. My travel alarm did not respond to shaking or whacking against the dresser, and I pronounced it dead.

The note was gone from underneath Lisa's door, but there was no answer to my knock. I called out to her, and got a muffled response to come back later. She was working.

Al was lounging in the hallway. When he saw me, he blocked my exit, his arm across the door.

"How's it goin', little Maggie?" His sour marijuana breath was in my face.

"Hi, Al. Sorry, I can't talk. I'm late." He didn't move.

"I hear you been askin' around about that missing girl. And then somebody messed with her door Thursday."

I fixed him with a tough-dyke, maybe-even-a-cop glare. "This place is bad news for a woman, or a young girl, on her own. But that's going to stop. Now get out of my way."

He backed off, swearing imprecations about unnatural females.

I sprinted to the car and drove home faster than law or safety permitted. Fifteen minutes to shower and find something to wear to the Sunday "garden party" at Sylvia Ericson's club. What a remarkably varied life I lived. In the back of my closet I found a vintage rayon dress from my thrift-shop retro period. It had a full skirt printed with giant cream-colored cabbage roses on a navy background. In about 1949 it would have cost a fortune. It had a few small rips, but none in strategic areas. I added the pearl earrings my corporate lawyer ex gave me last Christmas, and a favorite pair of high-heeled navy sandals. No hat, alas. Pugsley had been left alone with my one summer straw and within five minutes had chewed off its ribbons and dried flowers. I applied lipstick and blusher and dashed to the car, feeling equal to anybody's damn garden.

I scoured the area for fifteen minutes in a vain search for a free space. Finally I parked in the garage of the Barbary Club. While I circled around, I kept seeing the same grey Dodge van. Looked like I was still being followed.

Sylvia was at a table on the glassed-in terrace as promised, wearing a rumpled pink Chanel suit. With her was a stunning woman, who was perhaps in her late thirties, but keeping age at bay with every weapon at her disposal. She had a deep tan that might give her cancer. Meanwhile it gave her a certain glamour in a room full of cautiously pale women. Her ivory silk separates conveyed tastefully that she was rich. The only thing about her that wasn't tasteful was the huge diamond on her left hand. She introduced herself as Frazer Kearny, names I recognized as belonging to two venerable San Francisco families. She held onto my hand after shaking it, and murmured that Sylvia had told her amazing things about me.

Sylvia greeted me with a nod. After that she stared over my shoulder at the San Francisco Bay and drank her Bloody Mary. I made valiant attempts at three-way conversation. Sylvia replied in monosyllables and returned her attention to the view. Frazer gave me a conspiratorial wink: what could you do if your hostess chose to zone out? She asked blunt, intelligent questions about my practice, my background and my progress on behalf of Sylvia and Howard. I answered the former questions, evaded the latter and sipped dark-roast coffee. I wondered when food might arrive.

"I need someone I can trust for some very discreet work," Frazer said. "I hear that discretion is your specialty."

"I'd be happy to talk to you about it."

"Don't book any new jobs. I'm going to monopolize your time," she promised with a smile that transformed her face. My ex-lover Kristin would look a lot like Frazer in ten years. Frazer's mouth, like Kristin's, was set in permanently sullen lines. But also like Kristin's, it was a sensual mouth.

Sylvia roused herself to lift a finger at a passing waiter, who quickly brought her a new Bloody Mary. Then she tried to light one of Frazer's cigarettes with a slightly shaking hand.

"Honey, you're not very good at this dissipation." Frazer gave Sylvia a fond pat and lit cigarettes for both of them. She turned to me. "You look much too healthy to smoke, am I right?"

"I used to smoke and I still want one at least once a day."

"I won't try to lead you astray." Her glance put the lie to her words. Did she know she'd meet precious little resistance? Both of us were attracted and both of us knew it. Then an unwelcome vision of Sylvia with her hired lover Scott intruded. Professionalism, what's that? It was time to reintroduce my work relationship with Sylvia.

I spoke Sylvia's name. She didn't seem to hear me.

"Sylvia," I repeated, "are you all right?" She was still gazing into space. I put my hand on her arm, and she jumped.

"I'm fine, Maggie. Why do you ask? Howard is away, and I can pretend all the sordid mess outside doesn't exist for a few hours. Frazer and I spend every Sunday together, and we start out here. It's so relaxing." Sylvia wasn't relaxed, she was drunk and distraught. What was going on? I turned to Frazer.

"Would you mind if Sylvia and I talked privately for a few minutes? I'm afraid I can't stay long today."

"Of course. Watch out for her, our Sylvia is such an amateur about drinking." She moved gracefully to another table of laughing women.

Sylvia's hair was mussed and her lipstick smeared. When she finally saw her reflection she would be mortified. I signaled to the waiter to bring us a pot of coffee, and asked for a complete breakfast for three, the works. He gaped for a second, checked Sylvia's face for confirmation. She waved indifferently. The waiter straightened his shoulders and departed.

"Sylvia, we need to talk."

"I know. I'm so glad you're here. Talk to me."

"Yesterday I spoke to Beth Homan, a high school friend of Judy's. Beth told me that Judy was obsessed with her sister Wendy's lover. She blamed the lover for Wendy's suicide."

"But you knew that already. You said that high school teacher told you . . . ."

"She also told me that Moira was Wendy's lover!"

"But what a bizarre coincidence—"

"Please, Sylvia, neither of us believes it was a coincidence. I need you to tell me what you know."

"Did this Beth have any idea of what Judy was doing?"

"She couldn't tell me much. They hadn't been in regular contact for years."

"What a shame."

Sylvia, why didn't you tell me you'd been to the Capp Street house more than once?"

Sylvia covered her face with trembling hands. "That old woman told you she saw me."

"Yes, that's why I think you're better off taking everything to the police—"

"Maggie, I told you, there are reasons I can't go to the police! Please don't press me on this."

"All right, but your husband wants me to clear Moira of Judy's death. If you want to help Howard, it means helping me figure out what really happened. Will you do that?"

"I'll do whatever it takes to get back my life, *and* my husband."

"Please tell me what happened the first time you went to her house."

"She told me to meet her at a restaurant on Mission Street. She ate, I couldn't even drink my coffee. I tried to talk sense to her, to find out what she wanted, why she was so hateful to me. She wouldn't tell me anything. Afterward she insisted that I come back to that house."

"Why? That doesn't make any sense."

"For the same reason she told me to bring the blackmail money there—to degrade and frighten me. It worked."

"People in the house identified Scott as being in the house with Judy, but he says the last time he saw her was in Phoenix in July. Do you know anything about this?"

"Yes, I'm afraid I do. I was desperate when I returned from San Francisco. Judy was so irrational that I was anxious about what she might do. I told Scott that I'd help him get a job with one of my friends if he got the pictures back. He left for San Francisco immediately. Unfortunately, he didn't succeed. He told me she was belligerent when he went to see her. She seemed to think he was trying to become her partner in the blackmail. To be honest, I've been worried that he might have returned to try a more forceful approach, and things might have . . . gotten out of hand."

"What makes you think that?"

"I called his house two weeks ago, and his crazy mother told me he'd gone to San Francisco for the weekend."

"But he might have seen Judy without hurting her."

"You can't know how much I want to believe that!" She put down the empty glass and looked around for a waiter.

"Sylvia, are you sure Judy never mentioned Moira to you?"

"Of course I'm sure. How could I forget something like that? The photos had nothing to do with Moira."

"Then what aren't you telling me?"

"Trust comes slowly to me, Maggie. I'm already putting my life in your hands. When the time is right, I'll tell you more."

Several trays laden with food arrived. I found I had no appetite, but stuck a scone in my bag for later.

"Please eat something. It'll do you more good than that drink." I put a helping of eggs and toast on a plate in front of her.

Sylvia had drifted away again, and didn't respond when I said good-bye. She was slowly shredding a piece of toast, her eyes half-closed.

As I waited for the elevator, a jeweled hand grasped my arm.

"Is she all right?" Frazer asked.

"No, but you're in a better position to help her than I am. You said she doesn't usually drink like this?"

"No, she's devoted to looking perfect, being perfect, and let's face it, liquor doesn't fit into that scenario. But it's hard to know with Sylvia. I'd have guessed that she could hold a liter of Stoli and not slur a syllable."

"She said you're her best friend."

Frazer's mouth twisted in an expression I couldn't read. "I'm definitely her best Sunday friend." Then she gave me her full attention. "I'll call you soon. We have so much to talk about."

I pulled one of my cards out of my wallet. "If you need a P.I., give me a call. I am highly specialized—as an investigator."

Frazer gave an infinitesimal shrug. I was like an amusing lithograph that is unaccountably withdrawn from sale. There would always be another. She produced a card imprinted with her name and a phone number.

"That's my private line. Hold onto it, you never know when you might need it." She turned on her heel and returned to the terrace.

CHAPTER THIRTY-ONE

I was waiting for the elevator again when I remembered the conversation between the Women's Room attendant and the manicurist earlier in the week. I asked a waiter how to find the nail salon. His eyebrows raised as he surveyed my ragged cuticles. He directed me to the floor below.

The manicurists had a small alcove in the club's spa, behind an aerobics studio. Four women in maroon Barbary Club smocks looked up from their customers' hands and feet when I approached.

"May we help you?" one of them called.

"I need a manicure. Sylvia Ericson comes here, and she told me to go to the woman who always does her nails, but I forgot the name . . . Is it one of you?"

"Hi, I'm Lin." A tiny Asian woman who made me feel like a giraffe approached. "I do Mrs. Ericson's nails, but she don't know my name. You a friend of Mrs. Ericson?" She sounded like the woman I'd overheard in the restroom earlier in the week.

"No, but I work for her. She told me my nails embarrass her, and I have to get a manicure, so here I am." I smiled and held out my hands. "Can you take me now?"

"Sure, sit down over here." Noticeably friendlier since my social position had been established, Lin led me to her work table and stuck my hands in a bowl filled with warm water. "This your first time manicure?"

"No, I even had acrylic nails one time. Mrs. Ericson's nails are beautiful—are they acrylics?"

"Used to be gel nails, or silk-wrap. Now they all acrylic tips. She got full set." That meant that Sylvia's nails had been so short that Lin couldn't use a gel mixture to extend them, and she had to apply fake nails.

"That's funny. I thought the whole point was to grow out your own nails under the acrylics. Why did you cut off her nails?" This produced an offended intake of breath from Lin, as I had anticipated it would. Manicurists work to save fingernails the way dentists try to conserve patients' real teeth.

"She come in, her nails all torn up, nothing left!" As she spoke, Lin pushed back my cuticles none too gently with an orangewood stick.

"Too bad," I winced. "Did she tell you what happened?"

"She say man try to mug her, she scratch him to get away." Heavily lashed dark eyes met mine in wry skepticism.

"But you don't think so."

"She break *all* her nails. Did she scratch him one time each nail so much it tears off?"

"Good point."

"What color polish you want?"

"This tan one, please. I hate chipped polish, and God knows when I'll get around to dealing with my nails again."

"Too bad, your hands nice shape. Dark polish would look good on them."

I thanked Lin and gave her a huge tip, my own money, of course. Not a client charge, and not intelligence to be shared with the client.

✦ ✦ ✦

191

There was nothing I had to do, nowhere I had to be for the rest of the day. Restless, I drove to China Basin, where Judy's body had been found. It's a part of the city I don't know at all, and I got lost a couple of times before I found Pier 54. There was no fence, and I was able to pull the car right up to the edge of the pier. I got out and poked around. A couple of old fishing boats were anchored in the deep water. They didn't look as if they had moved in years.

Once the area had been an industrial hub of the West Coast. During World War II, thousands of workers had come from all over the country to assemble ships in round-the-clock shifts. Marine stores, cafes and restaurants had served their needs. Now shipbuilding had moved to other countries, other cities, and the shipyards were silent. The huge buildings were abandoned, decaying hulks, and nearly all the stores and services that had depended on the yards were gone too.

At midday there was little traffic. The place would be deserted at night. One person could have rolled Judy's body into the water in undisturbed privacy. It wouldn't take tremendous strength, even to manage the weight-lifter's discs the killer had used to weigh down the bag. They could take all the time they needed.

Judy's body might have remained in the Bay had it not been for a couple of eleven-year-old boys who got bored with fishing. They had stuck large, sharpened hooks on the ends of their poles and used these to poke into the depths of the murky water around the pier. One of them had torn a scrap of fabric from the nylon bag. Raised on TV, the kids had rushed to tell their parents they had found a drug-dealer's stash, the late twentieth-century version of pirates' treasure.

CHAPTER THIRTY-TWO

I went home to change my clothes. Liam had been there, but was gone again. No message. Time to try the Capp Street house again. I said a little prayer to Señora Morales' saints, asking them to ensure that Lisa would be at home and Al would be out of the building—or out cold.

The place was relatively quiet, only a baby crying on the second floor. No sign of Al. I knocked on Lisa's door for several minutes before she answered, wearing a dingy kimono. Her mascara had run from sweat or tears, and the purple rings under her eyes made her look like some exotic endangered species.

"There's somebody here. You can't come in," she said wearily.

"Come to my room. I brought a thermos and sandwiches."

"Sure, why not? He's not going anywhere, he just drank half a bottle of Cuervo." Lisa went back inside to get her keys, and a coat to cover the kimono. We walked in silence to my room.

I told her as gently as I could about Judy. Slowly, tears came, spreading the mascara further down her face. I handed her a tissue and she wiped at her eyes like a small child.

"I figured she was dead, but it's real now," she said. "We didn't save her."

"We were too late, Lisa. But you were a friend to her, maybe the only one she had. I have to ask you if there's something you didn't tell me before." She looked away, twisting the soggy tissue nervously. I steeled myself and kept pushing her. "Neither one of us could protect Kelly, but we can find out who killed her."

"All right." She paused a few seconds, then said, "I've got something she asked me to keep for her. You can have it, but I can't get at it now, with him in there. He's asleep, and sometimes he wants me all day—I don't know how long he's gonna stay. Come back tomorrow, and I'll give it to you."

"I'll come tomorrow morning. Meantime, is this the man you saw go into Kelly's room with her?" I brought out the picture of Scott.

"That's the guy that was in her room! Is he the one who did it?"

"I don't think he killed her, but he did lie about being here. Can you remember when you saw him—in the last month, or farther back?"

"I'm sorry, Maggie, I'm not good at that kind of thing."

"It's okay. I'll see you later. Meantime, be careful, Lisa. Don't go with anybody you don't know and trust."

"Wait, Maggie, do you work with a couple of big ugly guys?"

"No, I'm solo, why?"

"These two guys been hanging around. Dealers think they're undercover cops, and yesterday one of my tricks got so nervous, he was all 'Are you a cop?'—to me! He split on me before we even got to my room. Yesterday the same guys were in the hall upstairs, trying to act like they belong here. Al said if they weren't cops they had to go. They didn't show him any badges, and he kicked them out."

"If it's the same ones who've been following me, they're private investigators. I don't know what they're up to, but I don't think they'd hurt you."

"Well, I think I better get out of this place anyway. Guy who did Kelly may decide I know too much."

"Where will you go?" I knew better than to suggest any official options, like Child Services.

"Get on a bus, I guess."

"I know some people who work with kids living on the streets. I'll get you phone numbers for different cities, so if you end up in one of them you can get a safe place to stay and somebody to talk to."

"Okay, whatever."

"Lisa, do you know anything about the scavenger guy with the dreadlocks?"

"That's Pony. He doesn't live here, he just hangs out in the hall until Al kicks him out. He used to have a room here, and when he couldn't pay, Al took his stuff."

"Does he have a good grip on what's going on?"

"Depends on how much he's had to drink."

"Thanks again, Lisa. See you tomorrow." I packed up the clothes and bedding from my room and carried them to the car. Most of the smell would wash out.

Next destination: my office. I called up a social worker friend at home. She grumbled but gave me a bunch of referral numbers to give Lisa. It wasn't much, but it felt good to have something to give her besides cash. I hoped she'd land someplace that had a good service agency and connect with someone who could help her get out of the life.

After I had written up everything that had happened so far in the case, I took a break and called Jessie. She was unusually tight-mouthed. I knew she'd been to see her cancer specialist Thursday morning and was waiting for test results. Fearing the worst, I pressed her about what was going on.

"I'm good for another hundred thousand miles," Jessie said. So it wasn't that. Had I done something wrong? Jessie wasn't one

195

to hold back on letting me know that kind of thing. I could hear Tate urgently whispering to her partner not to "do it." Finally Jessie exploded at Tate.

"Tate, Maggie is a grown-up woman, and she deserves the truth." To me, as if I hadn't heard what preceded it, "Tate says I should keep my mouth shut, but I think you should know that Diana Hoffman was at church this morning with her arms around another woman."

"Oh." I listened to Jessie hyperventilating into the phone and Tate objecting in the background. I observed my hands picking an old piece of Scotch tape off the desk and placing it carefully in the wastebasket. A fruit fly circled the apple core at the bottom of the wastebasket. An ambulance shrieked by outside.

"Tate says it could be a relative or an old friend, we don't have the context for it," Jessie said. "I know you have a lot to worry about already with this case. But I also think you should know about Diana, so you don't waste your life waiting around for her . . . That is, if it was what it, uh, seemed like . . . ." Tate must be giving her cutting looks again.

"I don't know what to say. Thanks, I guess." I concentrated on keeping my voice as normal as possible.

"Oh, Maggie, it might all be for the best. I don't see how two people with lives like you lead, with schedules like you and Diana have, could ever make it work."

"That's what she said, more or less," I answered.

"You need somebody independent, somebody with her own life and a flexible schedule. And a woman whose social life isn't determined by the crime rate!"

"And you just happen to know a woman like that?" Here it came. In spite of myself I laughed.

"Tate's college roommate Lynda just moved to the Bay Area, and I think you two would be perfect together. Even Tate thinks it's got possibilities."

Jessie assured me that Lynda was a semi-butch independent filmmaker and political activist, not involved with anyone but not on the rebound. She didn't like to cohabit with her lovers, but she believed in monogamy. She loved animals. OK, she sounded hot. A cynical voice in my head predicted that she would use snuff or would insist on eating only vegetables that had committed suicide, but I was weakening. We agreed on a barbecue the following weekend, with a few other guests thrown in to take the pressure off. Jessie was thrilled with the apparent success of our conversation when we hung up.

I kicked the ugly metal wastebasket into a filing cabinet. It hit with a satisfying crash, and I contemplated doing it again.

Diana's stepsisters were under eighteen, but she might have birth siblings I didn't know about—or maybe a cousin? She could have been comforting an old friend or a fellow cop. People often came to the church in the Castro for company as they coped with the death of a friend or lover or a new HIV or cancer diagnosis, or getting sober. Maybe . . . .

Maybe it was time to get real. I had made a fool of myself when Diana tried to let me down easy. The issue wasn't commitment, it was that she didn't want to commit to me. I wasn't the one she wanted . . . .

I tried calling Liam at his job, my house, and finally his apartment. Sam answered, told me happily that Liam had indeed moved back home and offered to fetch him.

"Okay," Liam greeted me, "I was embarrassed to tell you I was caving in. But I'm happy."

"For now."

"Now is nothing to sneeze at, Ms. Garrett. Can you honestly tell me you're happy?"

I told him about Jessie and Tate seeing Diana with another woman.

"Sounds like she's making progress on the intimacy front . . . ."

197

"What a mean thing to say!"

"No, really, you're scary, Maggie. She has to start with somebody nonthreatening and work her way up. Give it time."

"Yeah, right. I'll be home later on tonight if things don't work out with you and Sams."

"Sams?"

"If I have to put up with him calling me Mags, he's going to be Sams. Goodnight sweetie."

I gave the wastebasket one more kick and went to a 1930s revival at the Castro Theater. The movie was about brittle, sophisticated people who had witty conversations about infidelity. The audience participation level was high, since there was a strong homoerotic subplot. A couple sitting next to me seemed to think it peculiar that I began to cry in the middle of it.

CHAPTER THIRTY-THREE

The phone woke me on what must have been about the eighth ring. I could vaguely recall a dream in which a telephone played a major role. The cats were stalking about, tails lashing, and Pugsley was barking furiously at the foot of the bed, bouncing on each bark.

I staggered to the kitchen through a gauntlet of cats winding themselves around my legs and a dog hellbent on tripping me. The phone stopped ringing before I got there.

Pod persuaded me that he needed an early feeding. "If you're any indication of my parenting skills, can you imagine what spoiled gangsters my children would be?" I asked him, passing the opened salmon/shrimp/cod combo under his nose for his approval. "But officer, they needed that Camaro. I'm sure they'll bring it back."

I filled food dishes, and stood enjoying the stillness. Except for the crunching of kibble the place was gloriously quiet.

It was only 6:20. I could turn on the answering machine and go back to sleep, spend an hour in the tub or dance around the cottage naked if I liked. Once again it was mine alone.

I settled on a cup of coffee in bed, and flicked the coffeemaker switch from TIMER to ON. Coffee brewing, I crawled back under the covers and gloated in the silence. Being alone definitely had its up sides. I threw off the covers and kicked my legs in the air. This reminded me of Cybill Shepherd kicking her fine legs in a hair dye commercial. The message was something along the lines of finding your self-worth by becoming a blonde. The only words I remembered were "Buck up."

Buck up, Maggie. I had a business, caring friends, the smartest animals in the Western Hemisphere. I could play a mean guitar, sing passably and type sixty-five words a minute, plus I had most of my own teeth. My recent mooning about Diana was interfering with living my life. Suddenly I realized that I was having an epiphany. Hot damn.

The phone rang. "Maggie, it's Chad Osafune. Did I wake you up?"

"No, it's fine, I'm just having your everyday epiphany."

"My what?"

"Never mind. What's going on?"

"I heard the autopsy results on Judy Simmons and I figured you'd want to know."

"You're the best. What did they find out?"

"She drowned, but she might've died anyway from the hit she got on the head. No sexual assault, and they say she fought back. There was bruising on her hands."

"Do you know how long she'd been in the water?"

"No guesses yet. You'd probably do as well based on the last time anybody saw her."

"Thanks for telling me."

"There's one more thing, only you can't let on that I told you, because the guys working the case are keeping it out of the news. She was wearing a ring with an inscription that goes something like, 'K, you belong to me, I'll never let you go—M.' Doesn't look good for your client, Maggie."

"You're right. Thanks again for calling me. I owe you, Chad." I returned to my bed and stared at the ceiling, thinking about what Pony the scavenger had said about the "big woman" who hurt Judy, until the phone rang again.

"Maggie, I'm so relieved that I reached you! I need to see you," Sylvia said. "I've just received evidence that Scott was involved in the girl's murder."

"What!" My head was swimming.

"Maggie, you have to help me. There's no one else I can turn to. I'm afraid to keep it with me—"

"What is it?" I interrupted.

She ignored me. "I'm afraid of what Scott might do if he found out I have it, but I won't let my family be destroyed."

"You should go to the police immediately!"

"They'll think I had to be involved, too! The pictures were of both of us, after all. And as you said, the blackmail victim is the first to be suspected."

"What do you want me to do, then?"

"Meet me at my club in an hour and I'll turn these papers over to you. Don't fail me, Maggie. I'm counting on you." She hung up.

The phone started making distressed clicks. I was still holding the receiver in my hand. I didn't believe Sylvia's story about being afraid of Scott. Even if he had killed Judy, I couldn't picture him as a menace. But I was very curious about the evidence Sylvia claimed to have.

It was hard to summon an interest in wardrobe, but the memory of the snotty staff at the Barbary Club helped. Wardrobe as armor—that was more compelling. I wore the severe black suit again, this time with a hot pink silk blouse. It clashed wildly with my hair, but I've always been quite fond of orange and pink.

The maitre d' at the Barbary Club didn't recognize me, although he had seen me twice with Sylvia in the past week. He advised me in arctic tones that Mrs. Ericson was not there. Moreover, he was not aware that Mrs. Ericson planned to be at the club that morning. He seemed to suspect that I was throwing her name around for the privilege of paying four times the normal rate for cold toast. He waved me to one of the fragile gilt chairs near his operations center.

"You may wait for Mrs. Ericson there. If she comes—" he caught my angry glance. "When she comes, I will inform you." He turned away to greet two businessmen.

While I waited for Sylvia, I did an old exercise my partner Jack had taught me early in our working relationship. He called it "Slice 'em and Dice 'em." The idea was to dissect the characters of key players in a situation to predict how they would act. He generally wanted to bet on the outcomes. Damn, I wished Jack was with me, even if his breath would have made the maitre d' swoon.

Okay, taking it from the top:

Sylvia claimed to have evidence against Scott Bentley, and he did have a strong motive. He denied coming to see Judy in San Francisco, but he'd been seen in Judy's room in September. Still, Scott only made a passable suspect if he was acting on Sylvia's behalf. Judy's blackmail had cost Scott a cushy job, and Sylvia was determined to get those photos back. She might have made him irresistible promises—or threats. On his own he had almost no resources, unless they were provided for him (back to Sylvia again). He was rather dim. Could he summon the will and wit to plot the details of a murder? Unlikely. Besides, his actions on Judy's behalf appeared to have been motivated by genuine kindness, and he allowed his embarrassing mother to live with him. In short, if he had killed Judy, I'd bet it was an accident. And I was pretty sure that he was the one who had called for "Kelly" on the pay phone outside her room the first night I was at the house on Capp Street, over two weeks after her death.

The most obvious suspect was Moira. The alcoholic scavenger, Pony, had said that a big, rich woman had hurt Judy. Judy's journal and all the stories Judy had told about Moira threatened her work and reputation. Moira would have been best served by a living Judy, proven to be a liar. That was, of course, assuming that Judy's charges were lies. But supposing Moira *had* killed Judy, surely she would have removed that damning engraved ring from Judy's finger. If Judy's body was never found, her accusations unsubstantiated, Moira would live under a shadow the rest of her life, although she might be able to practice her profession. Could Moira have done it? She didn't have much muscle tone, but her weight would be an asset in shoving a body off the pier. As for her ruthlessness in dealing with an enemy, it was hard to tell. For all her self-avowed openness, Moira was opaque.

Sylvia had a strong motive for murder, and in spite of her protests, I was sure that she had access to plenty of money. Sober, she was observant and intelligent. But half the times I had met her she'd been too drunk to pull off any action that involved planning. Or had she? Sylvia was accustomed to wealth and leisure, and her marriage to a doting but judgmental husband was at stake. I had seen her upper arms—she had better muscle tone than most women my age. Wrestling a dead weight into a car and off a pier would be within her capabilities. She traveled from Phoenix to San Francisco so regularly that she'd know the city well. She broke all her nails at around the time Judy was murdered and dumped in the Bay.

Howard Ericson was even more of an enigma than his wife or daughter. He had secrets that he wanted to keep hidden. What if Judy had picked up on these? Or what if, contrary to Sylvia's efforts, Howard found out about Judy's photos of Sylvia and Scott? But why pay me extra for advance knowledge about it? Then there was his determination to make everything right for Moira, the one who stood to lose most from Judy's machinations. How far would he be willing to go to stop Judy? Howard was extremely wealthy. His dealings with Robert Summers, the

Glass Agency and me showed his tendency to hire people to take care of messy, difficult tasks. As much as I disliked him, I couldn't see him bludgeoning Judy and dumping her body in the Bay himself. I could, however, picture him handing a packet of cash to the killer.

Outside the orbit of the Ericsons, there was always Jerry, the manager of Nature's Harmony Foods. If Judy had found proof that Jerry was passing off chemical-laced produce as organic, and maybe other scams, she could have demanded money from him for silence. That would give him a motive, but nothing else. He was an opportunist, not a player. Unless he was stealing from the till big-time, he wouldn't have much money.

Then there were the possible but unlikely ones: Al, the doper "landlord" of the house where Judy lived, or one of the other tenants, for that matter. Judy's fanatic father—what if he had molested her and she confronted him as an adult, threatening his holier-than-thou reputation? Or maybe there was another blackmail victim we didn't know about, who had chosen to take care of the problem in a more direct way than the one Judy had proposed.

After half an hour, the maitre d' allowed himself to purse his lips in self-justification. There were no messages on my office or home answering machines. I'd been stood up.

CHAPTER THIRTY-FOUR

I drove directly to Capp Street, my suspicion that I'd been set up as well as stood up growing by the moment. It was possible that Sylvia had taken a nose dive into a bottle and forgotten our appointment. Or that she'd been telling the truth about Scott, and he'd tracked her down. Maybe there'd been an accident.

Or maybe she wanted me out of the way for a couple of hours.

If I put my ego aside, I could admit that Sylvia had made a fool of me. She had presented herself as a sheltered, nearly helpless woman whose illusion of romance with Scott had been torn apart by Judy, and I'd bought it. I'd taken her boozing at face value. And I'd put Lisa in danger.

Lisa was waiting to give me whatever it was that Judy had left with her, probably the photos of Sylvia and Scott. Through my reports, Sylvia knew that Lisa was Judy's only friend. If Sylvia was, as I now suspected, Judy's killer, all she had to do was retrieve Judy's blackmail materials. That must have been what Sylvia was trying to do the night Señora Morales saw her.

I parked and dumped the stuff from my purse into my fanny pack. What was glaringly missing was a gun. As I ran from my car to the house, Jack Windsor's ghost started in on how many times he'd warned me to pack steel. "Shut up, Jack, it's too late," I said aloud.

Pony the scavenger came rushing out the front door, looking behind him, as I came up the steps. He crashed into me, and we both fell to the ground, then hurriedly scrambled back up.

"She's here, that big woman," he called over his shoulder as he ran down the street.

"Where? What are you talking about?" He didn't turn back again. I went into the house cautiously.

Lisa was home: The padlock was off the latch to her door. There was no answer to my knock. She had to be in there. Even when she went down the hall to the bathroom, she padlocked the door behind her. Of course, she might have a john in there, or maybe she was lying low, afraid that Judy's killer might come after her. Which, it turned out, was a strong possibility.

I called out so Lisa would know it was me, and tried the knob. The door was bolted from the inside.

The door was thin, but I wasn't wearing my Doc Martens, and I didn't have enough body mass to break it down. Whoever was in there had no way out except past me. Lisa's room faced an airshaft. I could wait them out, but what might happen to Lisa in that time?

"Open the door, or I'm calling the police!" I yelled, heading for the pay phone. The door to Lisa's room creaked slightly as it opened, and I turned back in that direction.

Sylvia Ericson stood in the doorway, a large revolver trained on me. She gestured with her other hand for me to come into Lisa's room. I stepped inside cautiously, and barely missed stepping on Lisa. She lay in a heap on the floor, her hands and feet tied. Blood ran down her face from a gash on her scalp. I kneeled beside her and checked her pulse. She was alive but unconscious.

"She'll be all right," Sylvia snapped. "I had to hit her. The little fool kept screaming and kicking—"

"What are you doing here?" I interrupted.

"I'm looking for what belongs to me, of course. After you

narrowed the field for me, it was obvious that Lisa is the only one who could be holding the photos. They have to be here somewhere."

"Did Lisa tell you she had them?"

"I haven't been here long, but I doubt that she intended to be helpful."

"Now what?"

"Since you're here, you might as well help me search. You're tall, you can get to the top shelf of that closet." She lit a cigarette clumsily, the gun still in her hand. "Stop staring at me and get on with it!"

Moving deliberately to keep from startling Sylvia, I placed a wooden chair in front of the closet. Jessie's most paranoid fantasies about my occupation were on the verge of coming true: I was about to be blown away accidentally by a deranged client waving her first firearm.

The upper shelf in Lisa's closet was packed tight. I stood on the chair and pulled down a grocery bag of sugar packets and other restaurant condiments, another bag containing cheap wigs, a ratty fake fur. Underneath that was a Macy's box, about twice the size of a shoebox. It was full to overflowing, and heavier than I expected. My hands slipped on the glossy coated surface, and the box fell to the floor, partially spilling its contents.

Sylvia poked the toe of her boot at a packet of letters bound with thick purple ribbon. "See what these are." She kicked them toward me.

The letters were from Moira Ericson to Wendy Simmons, Judy's dead sister. Only one, never mailed, was in an envelope addressed to Moira.

"Read that one," Sylvia commanded. It was written to "My only Moira" and signed "Ariel." The writer was almost incoherent, alternately demanding that Moira get out of her life and pleading with Moira to come rescue her. I was trying to decipher handwriting that had deteriorated to spiky scratches when Sylvia interrupted me.

"I think we get the picture. See what else fell out. And keep turned to me so I can see your hands. I don't want any tricks."

I pulled out a roll of pages that had been tightly rubber-banded. They were photocopies of receipts from produce wholesalers.

"Judy sure had the goods on Jerry," I murmured.

Sylvia gave me sharp prod with her boot. "Keep going. What's in that folder?"

If the receipts had been boring, the contents of a manila folder, which had fanned over the surface of the floor, made up for it. They were xeroxes of a "sealed" 1953 record of juvenile proceedings against Howard Ericson. He had confessed to beating and molesting numerous young girls. I handed the pages to Sylvia. She gasped, and the cigarette in her hand twitched as she paged through the transcript.

"Howard told me about this," she glared at me defensively. "Last month he came to me. He said a girl had contacted him, asking for a large sum of money in return for these transcripts. He cried like a baby and confessed everything to me. This episode of his life ended forty years ago, and he put it behind him. But not everyone would understand that. So I told him I'd take care of it, the way I always take care of him. As you must have guessed by now, the girl was Judy. Howard was so grateful. Men are always so grateful when they're allowed to escape the consequences of their actions." She threw down her cigarette and stamped it out. "See what else she had in there."

A grubby paper bag contained an old-fashioned velvet ring box. Inside it was a folded-up note. It read, "This ring binds you to me forever, To my own K—You are mine/I will never let you go—M."

Those had to be the words inscribed on the ring found on Judy's body. Judy must have planned to leave the ring behind as her crowning touch. Moira would have been made an outcast at the very least, if she wasn't prosecuted. But Judy died with the ring on her finger. How had the avenger become the real-life victim? Sylvia laughed at my expression.

"Judy and I were in on it together, hadn't you figured that out? Both of us wanted to get rid of Moira, and what a perfect way to do it, with her sainted mother's ring." She lit another cigarette and took a long drag. "It was a family heirloom, and Moira inherited it when Ellen died. It was easy for Judy to get. Moira is very careless with her possessions. The inscription was my idea."

"But why—"

"I've spent over twenty years cleaning up Howard's disasters, making him a success and keeping him one, in spite of himself. I couldn't take any more of his absurd guilt! How he'd turned his daughter gay by not spending enough time with her, and how he was going to leave everything that wasn't tied down by community property to his poor damaged, neglected daughter!"

"This was all a set-up to turn your husband against Moira?"

"It was Judy's idea. She planned to frame Moira for sexual abuse and slavery and then move to Mexico, leaving behind enough written material and gossip to end Moira's career, possibly drive her to kill herself. As you discovered, Judy blamed Moira for her sister's death. She took the photos of me and Scott to get my cooperation. She didn't need to threaten me. I was happy to get rid of Moira! Scott was right when he said Judy didn't understand people like us. Even idiots can be right sometimes." She ground out her cigarette on the floor, regret showing on her face. "It would have been perfect."

"But Judy changed her mind. Did you plan to kill her all along? My guess is that things just got out of control and she ended up dead."

"Did you also piece together why she changed her mind?" A

shade of respect returned to Sylvia's voice.

"When Judy finally admitted to herself that she was gay, she must also have figured out that while Moira may be a lousy therapist, she didn't cause Wendy's death."

"Very astute. Judy had the nerve to tell me she was going to destroy that made-up journal and leave town. But she still wanted money for the return of that molestation transcript on Howard, and the negatives of me and Scott. She thought I would simply pay her and let her go!"

"Why did you take the pillowslip from her room? Did it have your initials on it? Or maybe Judy's blood?"

"That's enough!" Sylvia pulled herself back to the purpose at hand. "What's in that folder?"

I pulled out a fuzzy snapshot of a man I didn't recognize coming out of an "adult" bookstore, and another, better, photo of the same man sitting at a bar with a drink in his hand. Could this be Judy's father, engaged in less-than-pious activities? I offered them to Sylvia, who waved them away impatiently.

I pulled out the folder of photos Sylvia was waiting for: a stack of eight-by-ten glossies. Sylvia Ericson in dozens of poses with her trainer Scott. In spite of surgical lifts and tucks, her body was that of a woman in her late forties. But this is not what made me want to drop the photos as if they were covered with acid. The pictures captured the brutality seen in certain kinds of porn. As Scott used her—bent in painful positions and performing acts that seemed to disgust as well as hurt her—his expression showed his bored contempt. Hers showed a desperation to satisfy him.

No wonder Sylvia moved Scott out of her life immediately when she was confronted by these images. Besides giving a vengeful husband the ammunition to cut her out of any financial settlement in their divorce, Judy's photos would destroy any illusions Sylvia had nurtured about her relationship with Scott.

Sylvia sagged against a chair, poring over the photos. I reached into the bottom of the box and pulled out a large manila envelope. It contained blown-up color prints, taken from different angles, of a suitcase with Howard Ericson's name on the leather luggage tag. The suitcase was opened on top of a bed. I recognized the distinctive green linen of the bed's coverlet. It was the same as in the photos of Sylvia and Scott. And it matched the bedding I'd found in Judy's bedroom. Spilling from the suitcase were Polaroid shots of little girls in absurdly adult, sexual poses. They were all naked.

Now it was my hand that shook violently as I thrust the photos at Sylvia. "This must be what Howard wanted to keep a secret from you and Moira. Or did you know about this already? Maybe you're the one who takes the pictures!"

"What are you raving about?" She tore the photos from me. "Oh Howard, you promised me it was over . . . . Oh, Howard, you spread this filth out on my own bed!" She bent over and retched, then covered her face.

I dashed toward the door. My foot caught on something and I stumbled. A heavy object struck my head with a crack, and everything went dark.

CHAPTER THIRTY-FIVE

I woke to intense pain centered at the back of my skull. Someone was saying my name over and over. The furniture in the room wouldn't hold still. With a huge effort I turned my head in the direction of the voice. It was the only part of my body that could move. For a horrible moment I was disoriented—was I paralyzed? No, but I was trussed up with what felt like twine, my hands bound to my ankles behind my back. Lisa was watching me anxiously from the other side of the room.

"I thought she'd killed you, she hit you hard enough. I'd just come to when you tried to run for it. I shut my eyes again, and she didn't come over to me before she left. Is she the one who did Kelly?"

I nodded and regretted the movement.

"She was cussing and talking to herself. I opened my eyes for a second and saw her throwing things into her tote bag."

"Did you get any idea of what she was going to do, Lisa?"

"Mostly it was the kind of bullshitting stuff you say to yourself. Something about going too far this time, and she wasn't going to clean up for him anymore."

"Maybe we should try yelling for help?"

"Oh, yeah, and have Al come save us?"

"Okay, let's see if we can rescue ourselves first. Do you know what she used to tie you up?"

"Yeah, it's an old piece of rope I used for a leash back when I had a dog. At least she tied me in front. I've been trying to saw it on the table leg, but it's way tough."

"See if you can maneuver over here." Lisa snaked her way across the floor. I rolled over, every movement an agony, so she could see my hands.

"What do you think?"

"Scoot over closer, I bet I can bite through that stuff."

"I've got a better idea. See if you can get the Swiss Army knife out of my pack here." Lisa unzipped it with her teeth. It took several tries, but Lisa finally pried open one of the blades. With only a few nicks to the two of us in the process, she cut through the twine binding my hands. Then I cut her loose. We gave triumphant whoops and high-fived each other.

Much of what we had found in the Macy's box was gone. Sylvia had taken all the photos of her and Scott and the records on Howard, as well as the evidence of his recent molesting activities, and the ring box. Where would she go now, and why hadn't she killed us if she expected to get away with killing Judy? Did she think she could still frame Moira or Scott?

Sylvia had padlocked the door to the hall. We were reduced to calling for help after all, but at least we weren't hogtied and helpless. I pounded on the door and yelled. There were sounds of footsteps in the hall. Surely someone would come help us. I stopped the pounding and shouting for a moment to listen for a response. Nothing.

"Try yelling out the window, Lisa!" I started swinging a chair against the door.

After five minutes of unholy din, there was a heavy crack of metal against the door. I shouted at Lisa to wait for a second, and heard Señora Morales in heated debate with Al.

"I break this lock!"

"This is my place! Nobody takes a hatchet to that door, long as I'm here."

"*Basta ya!* I cut you down, then I cut the door!"

With the crash of splintering wood, Señora Morales stood in the doorway in an oversized man's wool dressing gown, her braids partly undone, a huge meat cleaver still upraised. Al stood, wild-eyed and shaking, a respectful distance away. She dropped the cleaver and spread her arms toward us.

"*Pobrecitas!* It was that yellow-hair woman who did this to you, no? Come down to my kitchen, we call police, and I give you my *sopa de res.*"

I left her fussing over Lisa and staggered past Al into the hall. The addict I'd asked about "Kelly" a lifetime ago was using the pay phone. It must have been difficult to hear the person on the other line while we were screaming for help. I grabbed the receiver out of his hand and slammed it into its cradle. "Emergency—I'm calling the police. You can have the phone back in a few minutes." I stared him down and he left, calling me hideous names.

Miraculously, the 911 dispatcher answered almost instantly. I told her that Sylvia was armed and had already killed one person, and that I believed she was en route to kill her husband at the Fairmont Hotel. There was no answer at the hotel suite. I called Robert Summers' office and had to threaten to sue his secretary for obstruction of justice before she put me through to him. He had no idea of Howard's whereabouts. I told him briefly what had happened and what I suspected Sylvia intended to do. With genuine horror in his voice, he promised to do what he could to warn Howard and Moira.

My vision was a little off, and my brain felt as if it had been removed and inexpertly replaced, but I decided I could drive. Just pretend that you have the hangover of the century, I told myself. Annoying, and you never want to feel that way again, but you can still function. The moderate thunk of the closing door made pain bounce around in my skull.

Halfway to the hotel I realized I'd got it wrong. Sylvia intended to kill Howard, but first she'd go after her primary target, her stepdaughter Moira. The cops would be moving on the Ericsons' hotel suite. Meanwhile, Sylvia was on her way to Moira's office on the other side of the city.

I pulled into a driveway, made a fast reverse and headed toward Moira's neighborhood, watching for a pay phone. I saw two, both torn partially out of their fixtures, wires dangling. Would I have stopped at one if it had been working? I had already lost too much time already. Where were those Parker Agency guys who had become my permanent shadows? Sylvia must have let them go after she zeroed in on Lisa. I bore down harder on the gas pedal. If I was lucky, I'd be pursued by a squad car.

I didn't know what Sylvia was driving, so there was no way of knowing whether she was inside. A narrow alley ran along the side of Moira's office building. I pulled into it and parked, tore off my suit jacket, and belted on my fanny pack. All I had with me were my heavyweight flashlight and Swiss Army knife. I threw my car keys and knife in the fanny pack and stuck the flashlight in its belt. Mighty puny battle gear.

The garden I remembered seeing through Moira's windows was right on the other side of the alley, protected by a wall topped with wire and spikes. I stood on the car and scaled the wall. One of the spikes snagged my skirt and I wasted a minute trying to get free. I finally slipped out of the skirt and left it hanging on the spike. I dropped to the ground on the other side.

The rock garden was serenely quiet. A small fountain burbled in one corner, the splash of its water on stones the only sound except for far-off street noise. All of the windows facing the garden had their blinds drawn. I ran past them to what I thought must be Moira's office. The French windows were locked and the shades pulled shut. I put my ear to the pane. Inside, a woman's voice rose and fell in volume. It was more like a theatrical monologue than normal conversation.

Through the slats of the shades I could see that the lights in the office had been turned off. My silhouette might be visible inside the room. I moved past the glass, hugging the wall. Jack had taught me to memorize every room for entrances and exits. I remembered that Moira's office had another window. I picked up a hefty rock from the garden and slid along the side of the building. This window, set waist-high in the wall, was open. I crouched under and to the side of it and peered over the sill.

Moira sat bolt upright in her deep leather chair, her hands gripping its armrests. Sylvia was pacing in an arc a few feet from Moira. Her eyes never left the therapist's stricken face. It was Sylvia I had heard speaking. Moira was making sporadic attempts to placate her. On the floor in a corner of the room crouched the client whose session Sylvia must have invaded, an ashen-faced woman in a gray business suit, quietly crying and clutching a baby doll.

"All these years . . ." Sylvia continued. She had the revolver cradled in her arms. "All these long years I've played the good wife. I listened to Howard moan and groan about his darling little daughter, and how she went wrong after he took up with me. How loyal to your mother you were. How it must have been his fault that you turned against men."

She walked in my direction and I dived away from the window. I could hear her footsteps recede as she reversed. I stuck my head up again over the sill again. Sylvia was pulling the child porno pictures out of her tote bag. She brandished them at Moira.

"Tell me, I've wanted to know for a while now, ever since Howard told me about his 'thing' for little girls. Did you seduce him when you were young and cute?"

Moira gasped. Sylvia gave a short, harsh laugh and resumed

her pacing, the gun again held close to her.

"You didn't know he likes little girls? Of course not, in that way you are just like your father . . . hiding from reality! I've always thought it so laughable that you could pretend to understand anyone's problems, let alone help them! I know the investigator came to see you. Did she tell you that your protégée Kelly was really your lover Wendy's baby sister? That girl was on your trail for a long time."

Sylvia had dumped the blackmail items on the floor, and now kicked them toward Moira's chair. "Pick them up and look at them. You brought all this down on Howard and me. I want you to know all the details." Moira didn't move. Her eyes were tightly closed. Sylvia kicked photos and papers across the room.

"All right," Sylvia hissed, "you want to die in utter ignorance about the whole thing. That's your choice. Afterwards I'm going to have a talk with your lying, hypocritical father."

She clumsily assumed the two-handed firing pose.

I hurled the rock into the far corner of the room. It crashed into a shelf of dolls with a loud explosion as the light-weight wood snapped. Then I flipped the flashlight into the other corner of the room, where it smashed a lamp. Sylvia whirled toward the first crash, firing the pistol, then toward the second, making a 180-degree turn. Moira screamed when she saw me crawl over the sill. Sylvia swung back toward her. I sprang onto Sylvia's back, and we tumbled to the floor.

Sylvia was using the revolver as a club to beat at me as we thrashed about. She was in excellent condition, and her adrenaline was high on revenge, but I was younger and used to fighting dirty. After nearly getting my eye poked out with the gun barrel, I pinned her beneath me with a wrestler's lock on her head. Her gun hand was still free and she fired the pistol again, trying to angle her arm to point the gun in my direction. Moira and the client were screaming in fear. I might have been screaming, too.

I twisted her left arm behind her and sat on top of her. She writhed desperately under me, and fired the pistol once more. Still gripping her left arm, I threw my full weight onto my knee and landed on her right wrist. She shrieked as the bone snapped, and dropped the gun.

"Call the police, one of you!" I ordered the other women.

"She cut the phone line!" the client yelled.

"Well, at least that gives us something to tie her up with! Moira, disconnect that phone cord and hand it to me." She didn't move. "Moira—now, dammit!" She bent slowly to get the cord.

"I'll find a phone," volunteered the client, from the doorway.

Sylvia lay still beneath me. She seemed to be unconscious.

Moira approached me—and Sylvia—and stopped three feet away. Her eyes were blank, her face slack. Sweet Jesus, she couldn't go into shock now!

"Moira, this is almost over, we've got things under control. All you have to do is help me tie her up."

Moira looked down at the cord in her hand as if she wasn't sure what it was doing there. Slowly she extended the hand holding the cord to me, as far away from her body as possible. I had to lean forward to grab it, and as I tipped forward, Sylvia suddenly came to life and threw me off with a quick jerk.

I tried to roll with the fall, but my face slammed into something very hard. It took a couple of seconds for my head to clear, and by then Sylvia had regained possession of the pistol.

The door crashed open and four cops rushed in, followed by Howard Ericson and Robert Summers. Sylvia ignored the cops' shouts to drop her weapon, rose to her knees and attempted to aim, left-handed, at Howard. She pulled the trigger, producing only the click of an empty chamber. At the same time, one of the cops shot her, hitting her left hand. Sylvia sank to the floor sobbing.

CHAPTER THIRTY-SIX

The room was full of police, loading Sylvia into an ambulance, bagging the weapon, ascertaining that there was only one shooter. They were wary of me, and I didn't blame them: I was dirty and bloody, my tights were torn, my blouse was hanging in shreds, I had lost my shoes somewhere and my skirt was hanging on the fence outside.

Howard stood rooted to the spot, his attention fixed on the heap of photos Sylvia had spread in front of Moira's chair. Moira, five feet away, wouldn't acknowledge his presence.

The officer in charge at the scene announced that we were being moved to an unused office in the building to await our individual interviews with the investigators. As we shuffled down the hall, Howard and Moira were momentarily placed in close contact. He spoke her name tentatively. She recoiled as if he had hit her. She moved to the far end of the holding room. Howard walked over to the other side of the room and covered his face with his hands.

Diana Hoffman's no-nonsense cop bark came from the hall outside. I craned my neck to see her through the partly open door. She had her head down, and was nodding occasionally as one of the uniforms told her what had happened. I wondered how she would deal with seeing me here. Surely by now my name would have been mentioned. What would we say to each other? Or maybe she'd take the easy way out and avoid coming into contact with me at all. Now that the adrenaline had worn off I was aware of how much my bruises and scrapes hurt, and I was feeling very sorry for myself.

A woman cop produced a blanket so I could take off the bloody rags that had been my blouse. Everybody's mother was right. Even worse than unclean underwear, I had worn no bra. It wasn't a car wreck, but here I was nonetheless, naked in the midst of authorities. Another cop fetched my skirt and located my shoes, one of which was outside the window and one under Moira's chair.

The bureaucratic anticlimax went on and on. Each of us was interviewed, out of earshot of one another, answering the same questions, posed in slightly different ways, many times.

The paramedics checked me out, and a pediatrician from down the hall bandaged the cut on my collarbone and predicted that I would have ugly bruises from being whacked with the pistol and going face-first into a wrought-iron table leg, but that was all. He gave me some Tylenol with codeine. The pain receded, and I was able to pay more attention to what was going on around me.

Moira had managed to hold onto her purse, and was reapplying her makeup while she waited for her turn to be questioned. She kept trying to put on lipstick, but her hand was shaking so badly that she made a jagged red streak above her lips. Then she wiped it off and tried again. She was talking to herself. I wanted to say something to comfort her, but no words came.

I recognized a familiar female voice in the hallway. Impatience crackled in her words. "But of course you can make an exception! I have to see Maggie Garrett—it's a family emergency!" Frazer Kearny, dressed in a caramel-colored suede suit with matching lizard spikes, strode into the room with two officers trying to keep up.

Frazer knelt next to my chair. She ran her fingers through my still-bloody hair and oohed and aahed over my bruises. "Oh. Maggie, you poor sweetheart!"

I pushed her hand away. "Frazer, stop—that hurts! What are you doing here?"

"I heard what happened and drove right over."

"Sylvia's gone. I'm not sure where they took her. Howard and Moira are here somewhere . . . ."

"I know, dear. I heard you were injured, so I came here first. How bad is it?" She slipped her hand under the blanket and slid her hands up my ribcage. I grabbed her wrist to push her away, and the blanket fell on the floor. I was naked from the waist up except for the bandage on my collar bone.

"Cut it out, Frazer!" I protested over my shoulder, as she settled the blanket back over me, "Why don't you go see if you can help Sylvia? She won't have many friends left."

"Oh, you'd be surprised, Maggie." Frazer's hands massaged my shoulders, neck and back with a sensuous rhythm. It felt wonderful. I closed my eyes and leaned into it as shamelessly as a cat.

"Let me take you home and get you into a hot bath, and then I'll go see to poor Sylvia." I opened my eyes, sensing that Frazer's voice was being projected for someone else's benefit, and snapped out of my trance. Diana Hoffman stood watching us ten feet away. How long had she been there? Frazer continued to stand with her hands resting possessively on my shoulders. I twisted away from her grasp.

"Hi, Diana, I've missed you."

"Hello." Diana gave a cursory nod to Frazer. "Maggie, how is it that I always arrive directly after you've beaten up the perpetrator? Are you all right?"

"I'm fine now." I gave a her full-blast grin. Okay, this looked compromising, but I wasn't the one who'd paraded around with somebody else in front of God and everybody. I couldn't help it, I was glad to see her, and I wasn't going to act guilty just because Frazer had roaming hands.

"Diana, this is a friend of Sylvia Ericson's, Frazer Kearny. Frazer, this is Detective Diana Hoffman."

Diana turned to Frazer and the warmth she had allowed me to see evaporated. "Ms. Kearny, why are you here?"

"Why to check on our Maggie, of course." Frazer's eyes glittered with mischief.

"I see," Diana responded evenly. "Since you're a friend of Ms. Ericson's, perhaps you could shed some light on this incident?"

"Poor Sylvia hasn't been herself for months. She was being persecuted by some young woman, and she didn't want Howard to know about it. She thought she had to take care of everything herself."

"That's all she told you?"

"Yes. She started to drink heavily, which I feel certain led to what happened today. She hasn't been herself. Look at the way she hired Maggie and then turned around and found some other detectives to follow Maggie. It just shows how far gone she is."

"She told you she was having me followed?" I broke off with a yelp as Frazer stroked my scalp again and hit a sore spot.

"Well, no, I overheard her making a call to them."

Diana shot Frazer a look of undisguised loathing before she resumed her official cop expression and spoke again. "Are you telling me that you believe Ms. Ericson isn't responsible for her actions?"

"Absolutely." Frazer responded. "That girl and Sylvia's own dear family have driven her over the brink. Sylvia may also need a nice long stay at Betty Ford, but then, who doesn't?"

"Anything else you can tell us?" Diana said, her clipped tones erasing her accent.

"Nothing comes to mind at the moment, but why don't you

give me your number in case something occurs to me?"

Diana pulled one of her cards out of her pocket. "Thank you, Ms. Kearny. We'll need a statement from you later. Now I'll have to ask you to leave. This is a crime scene."

"Of course, officer. Come along Maggie, I'll drop you off," Frazer held out her hand. Out of the corner of my vision I saw Diana move toward us, then step back stiffly.

"Thanks Frazer, but I'm not finished here."

"Surely the police will let you rest now. You can make all those statements tomorrow."

"This is where I need to be, Frazer," I said, willing each woman to read as much meaning as possible into my words.

"Well, you have my private number. You can always find me." Frazer slid her hands down my bruised arms and exited at an admirable pace for a woman in three-and-a-half-inch heels.

CHAPTER THIRTY-SEVEN

Diana wordlessly handed me a large safety pin to fasten my blanket. We listened to the clicking of Frazer's spikes recede. Our eyes met. Both of us hastily looked away. Each started to speak at the same time, and then simultaneously thought better of it. There was silence for a couple of minutes, relative silence, that is. Crime scene people were joking among themselves next door as they examined bullet holes, and Moira was still giving her statement.

Diana cleared her throat a couple of times. "I'll give you a ride home after they're done with you here."

"Uh, I'd like that, but my car is here."

"We can have one of the officers drive it over later when they're finished. I don't think you should be driving." She squared her shoulders and went into Moira's office. I ended up having to wait an additional twenty minutes for her after making my statement to the investigators, but I wasn't complaining.

When Diana returned for me, she asked for my car keys. I reached for the fanny pack, which had twisted behind me, with a groan. Every muscle hurt. "Could you help me turn this around?" I asked her. She hesitated and gave me an unreadable look, but she did it. The pack was partially unzipped, showing a thick wad of hundred-dollar bills.

It took me a couple of seconds to realize that delivering the cash had been the purpose for Frazer's visit. I turned to the hunky cop waiting in the doorway for the keys, and held open the pouch so he could see inside.

"This is one more piece of evidence. The woman who came charging in here tried to bribe me." He bagged the money and gave me a receipt.

I held off my explosion until Diana and I were walking to her car. "Did you see her put it there?" I demanded, angrier with each second. "Did you think I'd pocket the money if I left with her? No wonder you were watching every move she made!"

"Hold on a minute. I won't have this discussion in front of the whole damned force." We got into the car, and sat in silence until Diana pulled into a bank parking lot seven or eight blocks away. She unfastened her safety belt and turned to face me. Her face was stern, the traffic cop who clocked you at eighty miles an hour, no matter what you remember about the speedometer.

"I saw Frazer put something in your pack, after she had made absolutely certain that you didn't have any pockets. Hell, you didn't have any clothes on!" Her eyes were blazing, and her accent thick. "If it helps your ego, she stuck the money in the fanny pack when she knocked the blanket off your shoulders. Everything she did after that was for her own—and your—gratification."

"Diana . . ."

"I didn't know what to do." She began to cry, which caught us both completely off-guard. I was close to tears myself. I moved to put my arms around her, but she pulled back. She blew her nose and continued. "I have *never* behaved so unprofessionally. Seeing her with her hands on you like that paralyzed me . . . I didn't know what her relationship was to you. You might have been involved with her already."

"Diana, less than a week ago I made it abundantly clear that *you* are the only one I want."

"Somehow that slipped my mind when you were lying back in her arms today." She cleared her throat. "To get back to the issue of my suspecting you, I want to be clear about this—I never thought you would knowingly take a bribe. I—I really respect your integrity, Maggie."

"Thank you. Was there something else you wanted to tell me about?" I was proud that my voice did not quaver, my tone remained level.

"Something else?" She gave me a puzzled frown.

"Some*body* else, that you were with yesterday?" My voice was rising in pitch with the accusation.

"Yesterday? Oh, at MCC! That was Ernie's sister Nikki. Ernie was one of my buddies from the Academy. He died a year ago, and Nikki asked me to go to church with her. She lives in a bigotty little town in North Dakota, and she never had a chance to grieve about him openly, because he had AIDS. Were you there? I didn't see you."

"No, my near-sighted spies were," I answered, wishing that Sylvia had put me out of my misery.

Diana took a ragged breath. "Nothing has changed, Maggie. There's no one else. You're the one I could see myself with—if I could be with anybody. I can't make a commitment now. I don't know if I ever could, and it's just not fair to you." She chewed her lip, started to say more, but stopped.

"Wait a minute. Why don't I get a vote in this?" I wasn't going to go quietly. I cupped her face in my hands. "Maybe I'd rather be with you sometimes, until your bloody beeper goes off, than nonstop with anyone else I can think of!"

Diana pulled away. If she could have moved any farther away in that big-ass city-issue sedan, she would have.

"Maggie, don't take this the wrong way...I've heard those words before. Three times. I don't know how much is me and how much is the job, but I'm tired of this story line. It always ends the same way." She swiveled back to face the steering wheel and rebuckled her seat belt. Eyes ahead, grim-mouthed and silent, she drove me home. It felt a lot like the last time, but today we wouldn't be making out for half an hour.

I remembered my epiphany of the morning about my self-worth, single or coupled, and lifted my chin. "Buck up," Cybill Shepherd whispered, and winked.

We were in front of my house. Diana got out and came around the side to open the door for me. She offered me her hand, and I extricated myself from the seat slowly, like a post-surgery patient or a ninety-year-old. I felt every blow that Sylvia had landed. Worse, I felt as if I had lost that battle and many more.

"I'll help you get inside," she said woodenly. I protested, but she ignored me.

At the door, the animals rushed us. Pod attempted his usual leap onto my shoulder. I dodged to protect my bruised collarbone, and Diana caught him midflight.

"Thanks," I said, taking the purring cat from her. "Are you off duty?"

"Officially, yes, but I thought I'd go back and get a head start on the paper work."

I dumped Pod and unfastened the safety pin holding my blanket closed. It fell to the floor.

"Maggie—" Diana objected, her voice breaking. I moved in before she had a chance.

"Subtlety doesn't work with you, officer," I whispered in her ear. "Frazer was right. Someone needs to help get me into a hot bath, and since you scared her off, you're just going to have to stand in for her." I pulled her into the bedroom and shut the door.

The cats skulked outside the door complaining that they hadn't been fed, and Pugsley destroyed city property by chewing up the blanket I'd been given. The phone rang every fifteen minutes until Diana ran out to the kitchen and turned off the volume. She also thoughtfully fed the animals. Damn, maybe she *was* the woman of my dreams.

About the Author

Jean Taylor works at a San Francisco law firm. She has also worked as a secretary, kitchen helper, interviewer for cultural anthropologists, volunteer coordinator, emergency room clerk and Marxist party functionary. She lives in San Francisco's Mission District with two monstrous cats and sings soprano in the Metropolitan Community Church choir. Jean is working on several fiction projects, including a third Maggie Garrett novel. She welcomes email from readers and other writers at JTaylorRED@ aol.com.

Mysteries from Seal Press

The Maggie Garrett Mysteries by Jean Taylor. Red-headed San Francisco P.I. Maggie Garrett has a reputation for quick wits and an ability to keep her mouth shut. In the first book of the series, she investigates a case of money-laundering and murder in a gay and lesbian political group.
WE KNOW WHERE YOU LIVE. $9.95, 1-878067-62-1.

The Jane Lawless Mysteries by Ellen Hart. The Twin Cities are turned upside down in these compelling whodunits featuring restaurateur and sleuth Jane Lawless and her eccentric sidekick Cordelia Thorn.
HALLOWED MURDER. $8.95, 0-931188-83-0.
VITAL LIES. $9.95, 1-878067-02-8.
STAGE FRIGHT. $9.95, 1-878067-21-4.
A KILLING CURE. $19.95, cloth, 1-878067-36-2.
A SMALL SACRIFICE. $20.95, cloth, 1-878067-55-9.
FAINT PRAISE. $20.95, cloth, 1-878067-67-2.

The Meg Lacey Mysteries by Elisabeth Bowers. From the quiet houses of suburbia to the back alleys and nightclubs of Vancouver, B.C., divorced mother and savvy private eye Meg Lacey finds herself entangled in baffling and dangerous murder cases.
LADIES' NIGHT. $8.95, 0-931188-65-2.
NO FORWARDING ADDRESS. $10.95, 1-878067-46-X; $18.95, cloth, 1-878067-13-3.

The Cassandra Reilly Mysteries by Barbara Wilson. Globetrotting sleuth Cassandra Reilly gets herself into intriguing situations no matter where she is—from Barcelona, Spain to the Carpathian mountains of Transylvania.
GAUDÍ AFTERNOON. $9.95, 0-931188-89-X.
TROUBLE IN TRANSYLVANIA. $10.95, 1-878067-49-4; $18.95, cloth, 1-878067-34-6.

The Pam Nilsen Mysteries by Barbara Wilson. Three riveting mysteries, featuring Seattle sleuth Pam Nilsen, take us through the worlds of teen prostitution and runaways, political intrigue and the controversial pornography debates.
MURDER IN THE COLLECTIVE. $9.95, 1-878067-23-0.
SISTERS OF THE ROAD. $9.95, 1-878067-24-9.
THE DOG COLLAR MURDERS. $9.95, 1-878067-25-7.

Seal Press publishes many other books by women writers, ranging in category from popular culture and lesbian studies, parenting, fiction, domestic violence, health and recovery, and sports and outdoors. To receive a free catalog or to order directly, write to us at 3131 Western Avenue, Suite 410, Seattle, Washington 98121. Please add 16.5% of the book total for shipping and handling. Thanks!